"Now that your dare is fulfilled, I guess you don't need me anymore."

Denver's grin betrayed the fact that there was much more to come between them. Starting any heated second now.

"Nope." Lindsay was positively giddy. "Used you up—now it's time to toss you out." She stepped forward. "This cowgirl is moving on."

He shook his head mournfully. "Been a good ride, though."

"You'll always be my favorite mount."

"Hmm, you're just saying that to be shallow and sexist."

"Nah." She touched his cheek. "I really mean it. The *wildest* ride of my life."

"Yeah." Their bodies met, his chest warm against hers. "There's one problem with you moving on."

"What's that?" She was whispering now, hot and impatient already.

"I want you to be moving on...top of me."

D0650476

Blaze™

Dear Reader,

February can be cruel. Up here in the frozen north, the weather can be stubbornly brutal when our thoughts are turning hopefully toward spring. Valentine's Day can be a day of love and joy or of loneliness and sadness.

This month the women of the Martinis & Bikinis Club chase away February blahs with their usual meeting, which includes sexually provocative Martini Dares, but also a surprise for my heroine Lindsay. She's off on the wildest ride of her life, thanks to sexy Denver Langston. Along the way she uncovers more Winfield family secrets and finally finds the key to real happiness. *Hint: it's not staying home playing it safe.*

Curl up with a hot toddy, enjoy the story and think about starting up a Martinis & Bikinis chapter in your town. Then let me know how you like *your* dares! Cool and calm or sizzling hot?

Cheers,

Isabel Sharpe
www.IsabelSharpe.com

Lindsay's Ruby Valentini
4 parts vodka
2 parts pomegranate juice
1 part triple sec
Splash of lemon juice

Serve ice-cold (with a warm heart)
in sugar-rimmed martini glasses!

MY WILDEST RIDE
Isabel Sharpe

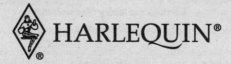

HARLEQUIN®

TORONTO • NEW YORK • LONDON
AMSTERDAM • PARIS • SYDNEY • HAMBURG
STOCKHOLM • ATHENS • TOKYO • MILAN • MADRID
PRAGUE • WARSAW • BUDAPEST • AUCKLAND

ISBN-13: 978-0-373-79380-8
ISBN-10: 0-373-79380-4

MY WILDEST RIDE

www.eHarlequin.com

Printed in U.S.A.

ABOUT THE AUTHOR

Isabel Sharpe was not born pen in hand like so many of her fellow writers. After she quit work in 1994 to stay home with her firstborn son and nearly went out of her mind, she started writing. After more than twenty novels for Harlequin—along with another son—Isabel is more than happy with her choice these days. She loves hearing from readers. Write to her at www.IsabelSharpe.com.

To my wonderful, wild and talented friends and writing partners in this terrific series: Lori Wilde, Carrie Alexander and Jamie Denton.

Prologue

Dear Daughter,

What a difficult letter this is to write. I am ill now and you are probably reading this after I am gone as it will no doubt take my lawyer some time to find you. It is clichéd but true that looking at the end of life makes you think about what you would have done differently. If I had mine to do it over again, I would not have given you up for adoption, no matter the cost. That pain never left me. But once my life had become stable enough to support you properly, you had already settled in with your new family. What rights did I have to you after all? This I would also change. I could have met you at least, and told you where you came from.

However, one thing I can give you now is knowledge of your three wonderful sisters, my other daughters. Brooke, your eldest sister, is two years younger than you. She is my most sensible, practical and gracious daughter, though I suspect a wild streak she has dutifully suppressed. Next is Joey, my brilliant lawyer, who believes ambition and strength can hide her vulnerability and rebelliousness. Lastly, Katie, my baby. She needs to learn to celebrate her impulsive behavior more creatively and constructively.

What you do with this is up to you. All three girls still live in Boston, where they grew up with me. I hope you will seek them out and make our family whole again.

I want you to know that not a day went by when I didn't look at them and also think of you, and the lovely young woman you have no doubt become.

Daisy Breckenridge Winfield

1

LINDSAY BECKHAM PUT DOWN the phone in her office carefully as if the receiver harbored an explosive. The calls from Gina were always surreal. On television blackmail was a dramatic high-stakes affair—threats, strong language, wrung hands and curses. Or excruciating, calculated and cruelly exciting.

These talks were bizarre simply because they were so ordinary. Gina was an old friend—or so Lindsay had had the typically poor judgment to think—so their exchanges were familiar, and while not exactly warm and fuzzy anymore, neither were they hostile. Gina treated her "salary" as if she were providing a service Lindsay should feel thrilled to purchase and chatted about personal matters as if their friendship hadn't taken this baffling turn several months ago when, in the middle of a catch-up phone call, Gina had blurted out, "Did you know there is no statute of limitations on murder?"

Wouldn't the press be interested to find out that a few years back Gina Nelson had seen Lindsay Beckham, the hot new owner of Boston's hot new bar, Chassy, kill her boyfriend? Forget the press, wouldn't the police be interested?

And Gina had gone on to point out, wouldn't potential investors in Chassy's planned expansion be interested to learn the woman angling for their money had run away from her adoptive family at seventeen and lived a large part of her adult life high on whatever she could find, going from man to man, searching for love and her own identity the least likely way she could find either?

Needless to say, after that the call had hurtled downhill faster than an Olympic skier.

The betrayal had hurt her not just personally but professionally. Gina seemed to know precisely how much Lindsay could part with and stay afloat. Lindsay wanted to do more than stay afloat. She wanted to take Chassy from the quiet neighborhood stop it had been when her wonderful employers and mentors, Laura and Scott Downing, had sold it to her for a song, to the trendy powerhouse she was sure the bar could be as their South Boston neighborhood grew and began to thrive. In the last year she'd made a lot of the right moves, including starting a local chapter of the Martinis and Bikinis women's social club. That guaranteed her loyal customers for its monthly meetings where lucky members were selected to complete wild and empowering dares.

With Gina back in the picture, clinging to her, her past couldn't be put to rest no matter how far Lindsay thought she'd moved beyond it. She'd finally wrestled away most of her guilt over causing her ex-boyfriend Ty's death, but she wasn't sure the courts would take the same view.

Unfortunately, Gina's timing was typical of Lindsay's life. For a precious few weeks in early fall Lindsay had started to feel she was finally digging herself out of the bad times and bad luck that had been her lifelong companions. A new vow of clean living, success in business, then the biggest surprise—information about her birth family—had been dropped into her lap the previous summer in the form of a letter from her deceased birth mother introducing her three half sisters, Brooke, Joey and Katie. Lindsay had invited them to join Martinis and Bikinis and was gradually getting to know the trio.

And then, kaboom, Gina.

There was always something. Granted, she'd made bad choices, but while a lot of people believed in the idea of happily ever after, and some people like her blue blood Winfield half sisters even got a shot at living it, for Lindsay there had only been struggling-ever-after.

"Hey there."

Her assistant manager's voice made Lindsay jam on a smile. Another case in point. Born into a wealthy family, Denver Langston had attended an Ivy League college and medical school, and had the luxury of ditching his lucrative career as a plastic surgeon in L.A. because the work hadn't been what he expected.

Now he had the further luxury of slumming in her bar while he figured out what he wanted to do next and where.

If she didn't respect him so much, she…well, she might not.

"Hi, Denver."

He moved toward her, early as always for his shift, slipping off the royal blue jacket that didn't look thick enough to ward off the dismal damp cold of winter in Massachusetts, but doubtless was several-hundred-dollar state-of-the-art Alpine gear. "How goes it?"

Lindsay shrugged and turned toward her desk, looking for something to straighten. As usual there was nothing. Though she'd always been teased for her compulsive neatness, first by her sloppy adoptive parents and her equally sloppy boyfriends, now by her staff, order kept her from feeling panicked and overwhelmed. And something about Denver made her feel both.

"The usual." And how screwed up was her life that being blackmailed counted as the usual?

He watched her with that dark gaze that lately was making her want things she couldn't have with him. Sex, intimacy, sex, fun times, sex…did she mention sex? Too risky. She was his boss for one, and not anxious for a sexual harassment lawsuit on top of blackmail, thanks very much. Second, she liked him, and whatever they started would sputter all too soon and ruin their working relationship. One thing she'd learned the hard way, men didn't stick around after the initial orgasmic thrill wore off.

"Everything okay?"

She nodded, sure she wasn't fooling him. Denver wasn't much of a talker, but he had this unsettling way of tuning into her moods that made her…

Well, she wasn't quite sure what it made her, but she knew it wasn't any healthier for her peace of mind than the calls from Gina.

"You're sure?"

"Sure." She nodded, aware her tone was too bright and he'd notice. "Fine."

"Uh-huh." Sarcasm became him. Everything became him. "And I'm Paris Hilton."

"Post-op?" If she looked at him any longer, her insides would twist up and she'd start with the blush-and-stutter crap.

Tall and imposing, handsome to a point, nose too proud to be perfect, Denver wasn't the kind of guy that turned female heads the first time he walked into a room, but probably the second or third, and definitely once he'd smiled and shown his easy charm. He was also the kind of guy that could intimidate most people simply by setting his jaw a certain way and scowling. She'd seen him in action when the occasional patron got rowdy.

Luckily it took more than hard jaws and scowls to get her to crack.

"So you're not going to tell me what's wrong?"

"Do I ever?" She glanced over to see him shake his head, amusement turning up the corners of his mouth.

"Nah. But I keep trying."

"Yeah, you do." She opened a cabinet drawer to look busy, wondering why he bothered, and riffled through the hanging folders searching for the file on the next evening's Martinis and Bikinis Love or Lust? pre-Valentine's Day party, probably passing it three times.

"This what you want?" He found the file and handed it to her.

"How did you know?"

"Same file you always pull when I come in here to talk to you."

Busted. She turned her head to hide the blush that was her fair skin's nemesis, which she could control around ninety-nine percent of the population. Guess who belonged to the one percent? "Thank you."

"Lindsay." His voice was too intimate; he moved closer and she tensed, ready to tell him to back off. "Would you—"

"Hey, guys, what's up?"

Saved by the bell. Justin Bell, their hot young bartender, hired at the end of the summer and raking in devoted female customers. He swaggered into her office, dressed in butt-hugging black pants and a black T-shirt, dirty blond hair mussed in a look that probably took him hours.

"Hi, Justin." Lindsay moved past Denver. "Remember, we're running a special on mango mojitos and passion fruit martinis for our Tropics in Winter night tonight, so be ready."

"Sweetheart, for you, I am always ready." Justin gyrated his pelvis and Lindsay laughed in spite of her crappy mood.

"Just keep the customers happy, Justin. I'll worry about keeping me happy."

He shook his head. "Lindsay, babe, you have got to get yourself somewhere warm. Miami or the Sahara…or even better into some hot guy's arms."

Lindsay raised her brows. "And why is that?"

"To melt that layer of ice you're stuck in."

Behind her Denver snorted. She shot him a look, then sent Justin a glare. Men. "We open in thirty, get to work. And for tomorrow evening's Martinis and Bikinis meeting, try eliminating the simple syrup in the pomegranate juice mix for the Valentinis. We have lots of women watching carbs and/or calories, and I thought they were too sweet. Maybe sugar around the glass rims instead."

"Yes, ma'am, boss woman."

She'd opened her mouth to correct him to *Lindsay,* when Denver's hand gripped her upper arm, making her hiss like an ambushed feline. She did not like being touched unexpectedly, especially from behind.

"Whoa." His hand gentled immediately. "You're on edge even for you."

"I'm fine. What do you want?"

"I just need a minute."

She nodded briskly, pulling out of his grasp. "Justin, if Casey isn't here in five, call her cell and light a fire under her ass, okay?"

"You can count on me, babe."

"Lindsay."

"No problem, Lindsay-babe."

She countered his boyish smile with a withering look and shooed him back into the bar, then crossed her arms over her chest and turned to Denver, who was leaning casually against her desk. "So, guy, what's up?"

He smiled at her imitation of Justin. "You want it straight?"

"I always do." She hugged herself tighter and had to

remind herself to keep her shoulders from stiffening up toward her ears. Not more bad news. Gina had hinted she'd be asking for a "raise" soon and Lindsay needed time with the books, time alone, time to let herself deal with the threat.

"Casey quit. She's pregnant and sick and can't handle the long hours on her feet." He spoke quietly but she saw the concern in his eyes.

"Okay." Lindsay nodded calmly, while her insides shouted, *No, not Casey, not now.* "She told you today?"

"She called my cell."

"Right." She banished the jolt of irritation at the idea of Casey knowing Denver's cell number and went over the schedule in her mind. "I'll work tomorrow's Martinis and Bikinis party. How long before you can get someone new?"

He shook his head.

She frowned. "That long?"

"No, not the new hire."

"What now?"

He pushed himself away from her desk and came to stand a foot away. She had to make herself not step back. "You."

"What are you talking about?" She felt like growling. She had enough on her plate without psychoanalysis.

"Don't you let anything out?" He put his hands on his hips, taller than her five-ten height by a good number of inches. "I picture this seething mess of emotions inside you. Like snakes trapped in a box."

"Why, Denver, how literary."

His jaw set. She couldn't help smirking. What did he want, that she'd break down crying because she'd have to work harder than hard until they found a replacement? She was born on a Saturday, "Saturday's child works hard for a living." She wasn't afraid of work. Work was healthy, clean and constructive.

So if he thought she'd lay her head on his big sturdy chest, blubber into his manly-man strength and allow that he was more powerful and capable and superior than she, he had another think coming.

Staff quit, that was part of the business. She marched to the door of her office and called out to Justin. "Cancel order to harass Casey, she's not coming in."

"Gotcha, big lady." He grinned at her scowl. "Big lady Lindsay."

She rolled her eyes and turned back into her office, feeling brittle and tenuous, as if one more push was going to send her over and maybe she'd need that manly-man chest after all.

Except she didn't. Life had taught her she could handle a lot more crap with a lot less trauma than most people.

Her private phone rang. She half lunged for it then stopped herself. Lindsay's panic would be immediately apparent to Mr. See-Everything. Then she panicked anyway and lunged again, encountering Denver's hand already on the receiver before she snatched hers away and retreated.

He had a brief conversation, watching her the whole time, a conversation that sounded as if another waitress was coming in late tonight, damn it. She imagined herself on the surface of the moon, everything bright, vast, calm, quiet, in the control of forces much bigger than her.

"Margaret's going to be late. Meltdown on the Mass Pike."

Lindsay nodded. "I'll cover."

"When was your last day off?"

"Don't patronize me."

"It's a simple question."

"I don't do days off."

"You need to." His tone was matter-of-fact, but his gaze was relentless. "You can fool most of the people most of the time but you can't fool me."

"Give me a break." She broke away from the hold of his gaze, busying herself with the bar schedule. She hated when he got sweet and probing like this. Hated the weakness in her he seemed to be able to generate, the small persistent desire to unburden herself. Why him? Why not her three new half sisters? She was starting to feel close to and trust Brooke, the gentlest, eldest Winfield sister, though she got a real kick out of spunky Joey and bubbly Katie.

She resented that Denver had such power and that resentment made her harsher with him than she wanted to be. Which she also hated.

Last on her hate list? That she had the feeling he understood all of the above.

"Come swimming with me tonight after work."

"What?" She swung around to face him. Was he

asking her out? In what capacity? As a friend? A date? "Swimming?"

"Yeah. Immerse self in water, propel self through said liquid with coordinated motion of arms and legs." He mimicked the front crawl arm circles.

She couldn't help a smile. "Got it."

"The neighbors are on a Greek island with my parents and let me use their indoor pool while they're gone. It's built in a glass extension to their house, so you can see the sky through the ceiling. You'd love it."

She stood silently, imagining the two of them alone past midnight, sneaking a wintry moonlit swim in a stranger's empty house and wanted to go with a force that shocked her.

"Um…I don't think so."

"Think it over."

"Thanks, really. But no." She managed to sound more sure that time, picked up an inventory off her desk and scanned it blindly. The paper flew out of her hands; she whipped around and snatched it back.

"One of these days, Lindsay." He was leaning too close, watching her too closely, undoubtedly getting much too close to the truth of her emotional state. As usual.

"One of what days?" She pretended not to know, pretended not to care, pretended to herself that he couldn't tell she was pretending. His chin was smooth-shaven, he smelled good, he was solid and masculine and everything she'd always fantasized about, excepting the silver spoon upbringing. Damn him to hell.

"One of these days you're going to let me inside."

"Or else what?" Her heart had jumped, was still jumping, like a maniac who'd just won the lottery. *Inside?* She knew what he meant but the way it sounded...

"No 'or else.' It's just fact."

Any other guy would get a sock in the nose trying such bullshit on her. But Denver managed to make the lines sound as much of a sure thing as his control over what he'd have for dinner that night.

"So what's your point?"

He smiled, unruffled by her rudeness. "So my point is that it's going to be good. For both of us."

Was he flirting? Did he realize? "You're sounding sexual."

"What?" He clapped his hand to his chest, brows raised too high. "No way, really?"

Her mouth opened, she started to speak, then gave up when she realized she was actually speechless. A blush crept up her cheek and she turned—or tried to. He grabbed her arm. "No, no, don't go, let me enjoy this. A reaction, my God. How I've waited for this moment."

"Hmph. Maybe you need more work to do."

"No." Denver tugged on her wrist, gently, the way she didn't mind so much being touched. "However, at closing time I'm going to ask you again, tonight and tomorrow and every night until you come swimming with me and I can get you to relax and have fun, even for an hour."

"Without trying to get *inside* me?" She stuck as much sarcasm as she could into the phrase even as thrills struggled to take over.

He winked. "We'll see about that."

"Denver…" She used an I'm-your-boss warning tone to cover her confusion.

"I'm joking, Lindsay. This is friends only. Friends blowing off the steam of the day in a nice heated pool."

"Yes, I know. I knew that. I know." She pulled away from his hand, furious with herself for imagining much more…and doubly furious for being disappointed he hadn't.

DENVER FINISHED ANOTHER frustrated lap and lolled at the edge of the pool, staring up into the perfect sky visible through the glass ceiling. He'd kept the lights off to enjoy the view. There was even a moon tonight, waning past full, white and pristine. The water was warm, the air cool, a large raft floated nearby for ultimate relaxing—how much more appealing could the setup be?

One way. But Lindsay hadn't showed. Not that he expected her to. He didn't even know why he'd bothered asking her, didn't know why he'd turned so stubborn about making her open up to him. Didn't know why he stayed in this town, at this bar, instead of trying to rebuild his plastic surgery career the way he envisioned it in medical school, helping people disfigured by fire, disease or defect, not hiking up the boobs and eyelids of vain rich people.

He'd been unceremoniously canned from one of L.A.'s most prestigious practices after losing his temper at a mother who'd wanted him to cut apart her beautiful and striking sixteen-year-old daughter and put her back together according to some bland ideal of perfection.

No, the mom hadn't invented the attitude, she hadn't deserved what he'd dished out. But she'd been the final straw for him and apparently, for his bosses. So he'd packed his broken-backed camel, driven across the country back to his home state of Massachusetts, parked his possessions in storage and his body in his globe-trotting parents' early-retirement house in Brookline and had taken the job at Chassy, intending to be there only a few months while he got his head together. Nearly a year later he still hadn't left.

At first he told himself he stayed for the comfortable routine, the excitement of watching the bar grow and change under Lindsay's skillful leadership. Then he told himself he needed a little more time, what was the hurry? Money wasn't a problem, his parents weren't due back for a while and he really hadn't decided yet where he wanted to settle or whether he wanted to return to California at all. Then he told himself Lindsay needed a friend. She'd been under some kind of extra stress in the last several months and refused to let anything out. He was a poster boy for what happened when you let discontent build too long.

All those were plausible reasons. Excellent reasons. Logical reasons. All contained a large grain of truth.

They just didn't tell the whole story.

And he wasn't sure he was ready to admit even to himself what that whole story was. All he knew was that his interest in Lindsay had slowly changed. Increasingly powerful sexual feelings were mixed with respect, friendship and, lately, growing concern.

None of it made sense. Jenna, his first love, had been a sweet petite redhead. With her he'd felt like Sir Galahad. After Jenna, his type became brainy plus voluptuous plus passionate, with eyes he could warm himself by, legs ditto. A woman with a healthy libido and a healthy grasp on her character and emotions.

Not some frosty blond beanpole with enough baggage to travel to Antarctica for a year.

What was wrong with this picture?

Annoyingly, he found himself in a position few doctors tolerated well—one requiring patience and restraint. He couldn't order her to let him in, couldn't give her pills for what ailed her, couldn't prescribe spending time with him as the perfect cure, wasn't trained to perform emotional plastic surgery to erase her internal scars.

He could only let her know he was there, willing to listen and to do what he could to help, prod occasionally, but never push or she'd get her back up and whatever progress he'd made gaining her trust would be undone.

Why the hell was he doing this to himself? Why hadn't he just found another red-blooded wild woman to make his life easier and a whole lot more exciting?

Maybe because he'd counted on changing his life by coming home and more of the same no longer appealed.

The slide of the glass entrance door made him jerk his head up and peer at the shape entering the pool area, a flood of adrenaline letting him know how much he hoped it was Lindsay.

The figure approached and he had to keep himself from frowning disappointment. Not Lindsay. Shorter, curvier, wavy hair. Adele, whom he assumed was another friend of the Robinsons.

"Hi." She spoke softly and came to stand at the edge of the pool. "How's the water?"

"Perfect."

"Perfect's good enough for me." She slid in gracefully, swam a leisurely circumference, then came back toward him, smiling. In the dim light her pale shadowed face made her look like the star of a black-and-white movie. Water droplets sparkled on her forehead and shoulders. She was undeniably beautiful—high cheekbones, almond eyes, lush curving lips. He instinctively gathered his legs under him as she drew closer, ready to move out of reach. The look on her face was purposeful, her eye contact pointed, but he wasn't interested in staying in temptation's way, because...

Because why?

He kicked off and swam a lap, then another, plowing through the water as if it deserved punishment. What kind of loyalty did he owe Lindsay? He wasn't supposed to date his boss any more than he was supposed to date his patients in California and he'd had no trouble there steering clear of any and all offers. Why hold back from Adele? Lindsay could be dating four other guys for all he knew. Was he going to keep himself away from all other women while she showed next to no interest in getting close to him?

Except...

He did affect her. He knew he did. The way she fought her attraction, tried to deny it and got so flustered, had only made him more determined to wait her out until she surrendered. That might sound cavemannish except as much as he wanted her to give in, he wanted what could happen between them afterward even more. He wasn't a hit and run type of guy—unless the woman made it clear that was all she wanted.

It could be all Adele wanted.

He pulled up to the wall back at the shallow end next to her, breathing slightly hard, probably more from emotion than exertion.

"Thought you were running away." Her low voice echoed in the glassed-in room; she flicked her fingers so water splashed his face.

"Why would I want to do that?"

"I can't imagine. I don't bite." She smiled and tilted her head coyly, wet hair shaped close to her head so her stunning cheekbones stood out farther. "Unless you want me to?"

"Hmm." He stalled for time, hoping the battle didn't show on his face. "That is an interesting idea…"

"Then how about it?"

"Maybe. Someday."

"Someday." Her disappointment was clear. "Not tonight?"

He sighed. Why not tonight? Why the hell not? Why turn down a warm willing female because of a cold unattainable one?

Because his thoughts were full of Lindsay tonight.

And the night before that and God knew how many nights before that or how many nights stretching out ahead.

As a doctor, he had to tell himself the obsession was unhealthy. Not to mention it was turning him into a monk.

"Not tonight."

"No?" Adele lunged unexpectedly toward him, caught hold of his shoulders and wrapped her legs around him. The movement brought her incredible breasts out of the water, the perfect rounds pushed toward each other and toward him by the astonishing mechanics of her skimpy top. "You're su-u-ure?"

He uh…thought he was sure. His mind had been sure, but his body was suddenly less so.

"It's not a good time for me. There's another woman…"

"At work."

He frowned. "What makes you think that?"

"Just a guess." She unwrapped her legs from around him. "What's going on there these days anyway?"

He shrugged. He found it strange that his job held such interest for her. "The usual."

"Seems like the place is doing pretty well."

"Seems like it is." He pulled back from her hands still clinging to his biceps, ducked under the water one last time and climbed out to find his towel. Time to go back to his parents' house. Talking about Chassy with Adele wasn't worth getting too little sleep for.

"I'll see you around."

"Sure." She smiled at him from the pool. One thing

he'd say for her, his rejection hadn't upset her much. He liked that about her. Attraction, dating and mating were all about success and/or rejection. Too many women took it too personally when he simply wasn't wired to want them. Of course he hadn't thought he was wired to want someone like Lindsay.

He raised a hand in farewell and started for the changing room. It struck him that Adele always showed up after he got there and always left after too. He didn't even know where she lived. Maybe he should ask next time he ran into her. In case he came to his senses and decided he could use a few nights of pure fun.

He glanced back one more time as he left. Adele was in the center of the pool, clinging to the raft, lips pursed in a kiss that turned into a fountain of water exiting her full lips. He grinned, waved again and she smiled wickedly, a half-naked, sexual-fantasy-come-true she-devil in the moonlight…

And he'd turned her down.

2

BY THE TIME TANYA SHOWED up for the Martinis and Bikinis party, Lindsay was ready, standing by the entrance to the curtained back room where their monthly meetings were held, offering a smile and a tiara with flashing red hearts.

Valentine's Day was nearly two weeks away, but she'd gone with a Love or Lust? theme, alternating garlands of red-and-white paper hearts with the tackiest Lust item she could find, a similar-size garland of shimmering gold-and-silver penises that made her both cringe and want to giggle.

The Valentine's Day tree, a slender trunk with bare branches painted white, she'd decorated with demure cutouts of wedding splendor—brides, grooms and assorted wedding loot—alongside models from a Victoria's Secret catalog and colorful depictions of a wide range of marital aids. Two bowls, one on either side of the door, were filled with favors for departing guests. One held white Jordan almonds tied in white net bags with silver ribbon and various "gold" wedding/engagement rings. The other held assorted condoms and tiny bottles of vodka, gin and tequila.

On the table against the back wall sat the Dare Box, a carved wooden box with a hinged lid that Lindsay filled with dares for the member nominated to be so honored that evening. All members of the nominating committee, but especially Lindsay, tried to get to know each woman in Martinis and Bikinis so they could select those women ripest for change and push them in whatever direction they needed help in going. Lindsay had successfully steered each of her new half sisters into the arms of men they wouldn't have otherwise approached so boldly. Katie and Liam and Joey and Sebastian were already engaged. Lindsay was sure Brooke and David would follow suit soon.

After her divorce Tanya had joined Martinis and Bikinis on the advice of her therapist. Since she was definitely the group's shyest member, Lindsay had gone easy on her so far. However, Sherry, the nomination committee's most gungho participant after Lindsay, had reported Tanya dropping timid hints about a cute new member of her lab team. When Sherry suggested to Tanya she was ready for a dare, rather than turning pale with terror, she'd blushed and giggled. Lindsay agreed. Tanya was definitely ready for a few more exciting experiments in chemistry than her lab made possible.

"Hi there, Happy Valentine's Day." Lindsay handed Tanya a heart tiara. It looked adorable on her, even though the flashing scarlet hearts clashed with her red curls. "I take it you're putting yourself in the *love* column tonight instead of *lust?*"

"Yeah." Tanya gestured to her midcalf red skirt and

white shirt buttoned up under her chin. She tried to look dismayed, but was unable to squash her trademark giggle. "I'm not wild enough to be lusty."

"We'll see about that." Lindsay gave her a wink and smiled when Tanya started looking panicked. The dares Lindsay picked out tonight had to be the tamest in their chapter's history. At worst Tanya would have to ask the guy of her dreams out for coffee or a dinner date. For most of the women that would sound about as exciting as an evening doing algebra problems. For Tanya, it was the equivalent of having to walk naked through the Boston Common.

"Happy Valentine's Day a couple of weeks too early, Lindsay. Hi, Tanya!" Sherry arrived, definitely lusty, wearing a midriff-baring white camisole and red shorts riding so low, they immediately suggested Brazilian wax job. On her feet, achingly high red heels that made her beautifully shaped legs look even longer. Every man in the bar must have noticed when she strutted past. Even Denver.

And here stood Lindsay in her standard bar black with sensible shoes. Ooh, baby. For a second she stupidly wondered what Denver would think of her in shoes like Sherry's. Even with them on, he'd still top her by an inch or so…

Enough. She handed tiaras to Sherry and tall elegant Lauren, who could be either love or lust in an exquisitely tasteful, strapless black minidress. True to form, she politely greeted Lindsay, then made a bawdy comment about the penis garlands, which nearly made Sherry's heart tiara fall off when she burst out laughing.

The women kept coming, close to the full thirty-member contingent. Lindsay handed out tiara after tiara, keeping a smile on her face, hoping her staff could keep up tonight.

Her smile turned warmer when three familiar and increasingly dear faces appeared in the line. Her half sisters: the youngest, Katie, tonight a very lusty French maid—the outfit in which she'd originally seduced her fiancé Liam thinking he was someone else; next Joey, equally naughtily dressed as a motorcycle mama, her favorite alter ego; and third, Brooke, the oldest—second oldest if you counted Lindsay, which Lindsay kept forgetting to do—who somehow managed to dress the right side of her body in demure bridal linen and the left in leather and chains. Love *and* lust.

Lindsay gave the trio a quick wave and greeted a few more women in line in front of them. After growing up the only child of parents who'd planned to adopt more kids but changed their minds after the supposed hell that was Lindsay—never letting her forget it—having half sisters was like something out of a fairy tale. Forget that the Winfield trio actually got to *live* a fairy tale, growing up adored by their parents, surrounded by money so old it probably built the *Mayflower.* For Lindsay, it was fairy tale enough that they seemed to enjoy her company, treating her as family in as many ways as they could. More often than she should, she resisted, feeling like the dairy maid among princesses when she was around them.

"Lindsay!" Katie gave her a bear hug. "Why aren't you dressed?"

"I'm working tonight." She gestured awkwardly. Katie's graceful exuberance always made her feel stiff and dull in comparison.

"Say it isn't so." Joey came up for her hug. "We wanted you to be able to party with us."

"Absolutely." Brooke's turn, her hug was also affectionate, as was the kiss she planted on Lindsay's cheek. A few months earlier Brooke had discovered John Winfield wasn't her father by blood. The girls' late mother, Daisy, apparently had something of a past, since the four girls had three fathers. One for Lindsay, who was given up for adoption. One for Brooke, who Daisy kept since she was marrying into the Winfield family while pregnant with her. Then the late John Winfield had fathered Joey and Katie.

Lindsay sympathized with Brooke. Not only did she have to deal with a shock similar to Lindsay finding out last summer she was adopted—shock tempered with relief that the selfish parents who raised her weren't related by blood—but the discovery meant Brooke wasn't a true Winfield. Purely symbolic since she was raised to be one, but that detail and their shared physical characteristics—a widow's peak hairline, wide mouths, high cheekbones and long narrow fingers obviously inherited from their mother's side of the family—made Brooke more approachable.

Lindsay handed her a tiara, annoyed at herself for not feeling comfortable enough to return the kiss. Her half sisters must consider her pretty cold. "Love the half-and-half costume, Brooke."

"Thanks." She grinned and struck a pose. "I swing both ways."

Katie rolled her eyes. "We'll hear that line all night. What's the 'tini flavor this month? It looks red and de-e-licious."

"A Ruby Valentini. Vodka, pomegranate juice, Triple Sec and lemon."

"Ooh, sign me up for that action. You sure you can't hang with us, Lindsay?"

"You have to!" Brooke said. "Tell the members to get their drinks at the bar so you can relax."

"No, no. I can't." Lindsay shook her head emphatically. She loved the Martinis and Bikinis events but as the organizer and observer, needed to keep her distance. She always had something to do, somewhere to be, a duty to perform. Besides, drinking had landed her in so much trouble so many times she couldn't equate it with fun anymore. "I don't mind working."

"We'll see about that." Brooke winked at her sisters, who grinned slyly back. "Right now I'm up for checking out the costumes and the booze. Who's with me?"

The three women moved past Lindsay so she could continue welcoming guests. By eight-fifteen even the latecomers had arrived. She helped Margaret pass around trays loaded with Valentinis, which were being consumed in generous quantities.

Miraculously, even though the rest of the bar had

filled up nicely as well, the evening seemed to be going smoothly. Justin had entered that state of fierce concentration where he appeared to be making five drinks at once. He'd been the best hire she'd made except for Denver, who wasn't sitting down on the job either, serving drinks, keeping the appetizers flowing from the kitchen—in short, filling in wherever he could be useful without any direction from her.

Just before nine they intersected at the end of the bar, Denver's arms loaded with dirty plates, her own carrying a tray of fresh drinks Justin had conjured in record time.

"Surviving?" He looked at her the way he always did, like he was trying to see past the surface, dark eyes calm and thoughtful in spite of his hurried pace.

"You bet." She steadied the tray, unable to look away from him. "You?"

"Fine. Seems like a good time all around." He smiled and moved away. She let herself look after him for a few stolen seconds before she went to rejoin the party—and encountered her three smirking half sisters.

"What?" She stopped cold, suddenly vulnerable and uncomfortable.

"My, my. I haven't seen that many sparks since the Fourth of July." Joey took a sip of her drink and moved to Lindsay's right.

"Looked *awfully* warm in that part of the bar." Katie moved to her left.

"I'm sorry, what's that puddle at your feet?" Brooke took the center position. "Could you by any chance be melting?"

Busted. The blush came on full force and busted her even worse. "He's my employee. Nothing more."

"Uh-huh."

"Right."

"Oh, sure."

"A damn good employee." She stood her ground, pretty sure the battle was lost already. "One I don't want to lose by doing any of the things you three are thinking."

"Oh, I don't think quitting would be on his mind. It certainly wasn't just now." Joey nudged Brooke, who nudged Katie who nodded as if she'd received some important signal.

Lindsay's alarm bells started chiming. Her half sisters were lovely, well-bred women, all capable of deep mischief. Lindsay didn't mind dishing it out, but like any control freak she didn't like taking it. "Okay. What's going on?"

"Isn't it nearly time for tonight's Martini Dares?" Katie spoke way too casually.

"Why I believe it is." Joey took the tray from Lindsay. "I'll deliver these. You're needed front and center."

"You certainly are." Brooke took Lindsay's arm and led her over to the wooden box. "Do your stuff."

Lindsay took her place in front of the table facing the glittering, flashing-tiara-wearing revelers. Something wasn't going to go according to plan tonight. Whatever the disruption, she hoped it was over soon and with minimal embarrassment.

"Okay, ladies." She waited for the alcohol-fueled chatter to respond to various "Shhs" circulating the room.

"Happy Valentine's Day and whatever else you're celebrating in a loving or lusty way this month. We've reached that part of the evening where members of our group chosen by the nominating committee pick out a scroll from the sacred Dare Box. As always, we recite the rules first." She pretended to unroll a parchment and held the invisible rules in front of her. "The members chosen for Martini Dares must be approved by a majority of the membership present. As you swore when you joined Martinis and Bikinis once you agree to pick a dare, there is no backing out. Period. Even quitting the group does not exempt you from your most serious obligation."

"Okay. Now." She raised her arm high above her head. "Show of hands that you have heard and understood?"

Hands shot in the air, including Tanya's and Natalie's, she was glad to see.

"Then by the completely nonimportant authority vested in me by the Martinis and Bikinis organization, I announce that this month's dares will be taken by Natalie…."

She paused, to let the crowd react, and to wink at Natalie who had her hands clapped to her cheeks, laughing along with everyone else.

Lindsay smiled. These women were such a bright spot in her life. "And second to pick her dare tonight is—"

"Lindsay." Three voices shouted her name as soon as she opened her mouth to call out Tanya's.

"What?" She whipped around to stare at Brooke, Joey and Katie.

"Your turn tonight." Brooke gestured to the box. "It's time. Right ladies?"

"I—" Lindsay's response was drowned out by approximately thirty roars of *Yes!* "No, it's not my turn."

"*We* say it is." This from Katie accompanied by firm nods from Brooke and Joey.

Lindsay forced herself to stay calm. "I've already pick—"

"Overruled. Unanimously approved by the membership." Lawyer Joey pointed sternly to the box. "Choose your fate."

Lindsay glanced frantically around the room. People might suspect, but no one knew for sure that the dares were planted. Tonight's dares were all geared for shy girls like Natalie and especially Tanya dreaming of her new lab team member. If Lindsay chose a dare now she'd have to think up another one next month mild enough for Tanya but challenging enough to whoever else was nominated to pick since shy girls were admittedly in short supply in the group. Coffee and dinner were barely the stuff of Martinis and Bikinis legend.

She opened her mouth to protest.

"No buts," Katie said.

"Pick," Joey ordered.

"Go for it," someone called out and the phrase echoed around the room.

Lindsay sighed. Okay, fine. She had no trouble recognizing a lost cause when it was surrounding her, full of stubborn goodwill as this one was. So she'd pick the scroll, have a cuppa with Denver after work or add a sandwich and call it dinner, take a nighttime stroll or whatever else she'd put in the box and end it. Damn, she'd really wanted to help push Tanya toward some happiness.

"Fine. I give in. Do I have to go first?"

The crowd answered in no uncertain terms.

Lindsay smiled and closed her eyes as Brooke led her to the box and guided her hand in among the ribbon-tied scrolls Lindsay had assembled in the wee hours of the morning. She groped briefly, aiming for the right corner, where the coffee date scrolls should be. "Got one."

Cheering, the crowd craned forward eagerly. Lindsay held the scroll teasingly aloft. "Anyone want to know what it says?"

The resulting roar made her laugh. She unrolled the paper, prepared for the familiar words.

They weren't there.

She read, read again, read a third time, her laughter choking into dread. *Oh no.*

Her arms dropped. She looked up at her half sisters, each wearing a knowing grin, though Brooke's was slightly anxious.

They were onto her. They knew she planted the scrolls. Somehow they'd gotten to the box and had changed them to much bawdier dares, similar to the one clenched in her hand.

"Read it!" someone shouted.

"Look at her face. It must be good," added another voice.

Lindsay forced a smile, afraid she was either going

to cry or throw up or both. She brought the paper up again with shaking hands and read out loud.

"Seduce the man you're most attracted to. Tonight."

LINDSAY SAT WITH HER HALF SISTERS in her favorite part of Chassy, a curtained small room off the main bar lined with banquettes on the sides and with four tiny tables in the center. The main attraction was a fireplace on the outer wall. At this time of year when cold reigned supreme outdoors no matter how ready the inhabitants were for spring, the room was cozy, intimate and relatively quiet. Especially now near closing when the music had been downshifted and the volume pulled back. Only a few stragglers remained at the bar.

The last of the Martinis and Bikinis club had departed ten minutes earlier. Brooke had called a private powwow before her sisters left.

"Lindsay, I just wanted you to know that all of us know exactly how you're feeling right now."

"Amen." Joey nodded vigorously. "When I pulled the slip saying I had to reveal my deepest darkest secret to Sebastian…"

"And when I found out I had to strip in public…" Brooke shuddered comically.

"And when I found out I had to have sex in a forbidden place…" Katie's attempt at looking horrified failed as her features turned dreamy and distant.

"Katie, stay with us here." Brooke snapped her fingers in front of her sister's face, then focused again on Lindsay. "The point is we've each lived the same stomach-curling—"

"Head-throbbing—"

"Teeth-clenching—"

"—dread that you are." Brooke grinned. "Any of this sounding familiar?"

Lindsay released her jaw and put a hand to her throbbing head, acutely aware of her stomach's distress. "Yes."

"So we're here to tell you that it's all going to be okay."

Lindsay nodded. Right. Everything was going to be okay. Everything always was okay if you were a Winfield. She knew firsthand that wanting things to be okay did not always make them okay. Yet she was the reason her half sisters all had to do those frightening and difficult dares. She'd played the bold matchmaker the same way they were doing now. And there was no way she could let them down not playing by the same rules they'd played by.

She just couldn't bear it if Denver turned her down. Or worse, if he let her seduce him and then disappeared, or let her seduce him and took over her life. Or—

"Right now you're going over every possible thing that could go wrong, aren't you?"

Lindsay laughed unwillingly and nodded at Katie.

"Oh, I was soooo there."

"I don't think anything will go wrong. We all saw the way he was looking at you. He'll jump at the chance to, um, get to know you better."

The sisters burst out laughing at Brooke's careful wording.

"What guy wouldn't?" Joey's playful words froze

Lindsay's smile. Right. She'd experienced too many guys that would. This time she wanted…

Wait. She wanted to be more than that to Denver? She knew where that led. When she fell for a guy she lost herself, let him run all over her, control her, then he'd leave and break her heart. Only Ty had stayed, but his control had become more and more extreme until it became dangerous.

No feelings could enter into this seduction. The only way she'd survive would be to stay as icily detached as possible. Then if Denver rejected her, whether before or after, it wouldn't hurt. She'd stay untouched. She had to make sure that sex between them didn't matter.

Even better, what if the sex really didn't matter? The dare hadn't mentioned Denver by name. The sisters assumed, but what if…

"I was thinking…"

"Yes?" Her half sisters leaned eagerly forward.

Lindsay's mind spun. Would it be a mistake or simply the lesser of two evils? "You know, Justin is actually hotter than Denver. I've always thought he was—"

"Oh right."

"Pleez."

"Don't even try."

She made a face. Okay, so Winfields were too smart to be fooled that easily. The dare had said the man she was most attracted to. Denver might as well be a magnet tuned in for her polarity.

"Lindsay?" Her personal magnet appeared at the

curtained doorway and Lindsay's heart pounded so painfully she nearly winced. "Hey, Brooke, Joey, Katie."

"Hi-i-i, *Den*-ver." The three made his name come out like a singsong grade school chant.

He grinned. "Did you have a good time tonight?"

"Oh yes." Brooke got up and sent her sisters significant looks. "We had a great time, didn't we."

"A most excellent time. Lindsay will have to tell you all about it." Katie got up. "Because we're going home now."

"Yes, we are. We had tons o' fun." Joey blinked demurely at Denver. "But not as much fun as *you* are go—"

"*Thanks* for staying." Lindsay sent Joey a murderous look she knew would make her most outspoken sister laugh. The three women hugged Lindsay with their usual warmth. She managed to hug back, feeling as if she were saying final farewells before her trip to the gallows.

"Relax and have fun," Brooke whispered. "I think he really cares about you."

She nodded dumbly. That concept scared her the most. Cared about her how? As a friend? Little sister? Or more…

All of it scared her. Looking back on her life, on the emotional and physical abuse, the fear running away from the only home she'd known, the stupid things she'd done in fast succession after that, all of which had gone horribly wrong, the terror of exposure from Gina for Ty's death…all that, and she didn't think she'd ever felt quite this frightened in her life.

Denver waved at the trio and turned back to Lindsay. The firelight flickered over his face making him look strong and dangerous. The room felt suddenly hot and way too small. "Seems like everything went great tonight."

"Yes. Yes. Amazingly well." Her voice sounded high and slightly panicked. She suddenly felt as if she had too many hands, and no place to put them. "Thanks for your help."

"It's my job, Lindsay."

"I know, but…well, I mean it doesn't have to be your job and you do it really well and so I wanted you to know that—" Geez. She might be many things, but babbling fool didn't usually make the list. "—so I appreciate it."

"Uh-huh." He narrowed his eyes, staring unrelentingly. "You okay?"

"Why wouldn't I be okay?"

"I have no idea. But you're acting funny."

Yeah, she was a laugh riot. "Sorry to hear that."

"Anything happen? With your sisters?"

Way too much. "Everything's fine."

"I see." He tightened his lips. "And that's why you look as if you just lost your best friend."

"Honestly, Denver. I'm fine. My half sisters are fine. Everything is fine." She waved a hand in exasperation, aware that this was not the most auspicious beginning for a seduction. "I have not lost my best friend."

But after what had to happen tonight, she was desperately afraid she would.

3

"THANKS. YOU CAN JUST PUT them there." Lindsay pointed to the corner of the living room in her beautiful two-bedroom apartment upstairs from Chassy. A far cry from any living situation she'd ever had. She couldn't count the number of couches she'd slept on, the roach-infested tiny rooms she'd shared, the basements she'd crashed in after leaving her parents' home. As much as that life seemed at times to have been lived by someone else, she still had to remind herself frequently that this beautiful place actually belonged to her.

Scott and Laura Downing, the couple who sold her the building for next to nothing, had been fastidious owners. She hadn't had to do anything but paint the walls, all of which had been shades of white much too demure for her taste. A strange combination of eagerness and reluctance to put down roots—not to mention spend money—had gotten her about halfway to furnishing the place. Finally she could describe it as spare instead of empty. A small victory, but a victory nonetheless.

She had to admit the place looked good with Denver

in it. She'd lured him up by asking for help carrying boxes of table lamps and pictures left over from when the bar had belonged to the Downings. The boxes weren't bothering anyone piled at the back of the storeroom downstairs, but she had to entice Denver up on some pretext and she wasn't going to suggest etchings.

Her first plan had been to jump him downstairs and get it over with, but she'd never be able to behave normally at work if the desk or table or chair they were near held such an erotic connotation.

Better up here or maybe in the guest room, which Scott and Laura had left furnished since their condo in Naples was one bedroom smaller. Or perhaps on the new couch in the living room where she'd ask him to sit. She rarely went into the guest room, which made it a good choice. However, the couch didn't invite longterm occupancy the way a bed did.

Okay. The couch.

So. On with the show. She could fake it, of course, have Denver go back downstairs with nothing more than a friendly g'bye and tell her half sisters and the rest of the girls that they'd been at it all night long, but lying wasn't her thing. Brooke, Joey and Katie would be on to her in a heartbeat once they started demanding details. In any case, her newfound sense of honor and her enjoyment of the whole Martinis and Bikinis concept wouldn't let her get away with that for long.

Best just to go for the kill. Close her eyes and think of Boston. The only way she'd get through the seduction of Denver Langston intact was by not allowing herself to care. Nothing good had ever come from her letting down her guard with men. Nothing.

"All set." He straightened, having set the box next to her most recent acquisition, the burgundy microfiber couch. It had cost way too much but made a fabulous accent in front of the dark orangey-yellow wall. The perfect place to get down and dirty for a quick half hour or so.

"Great, thank you." Three…two…one… "Would you like a drink, Denver?"

Blast off.

Her words—maybe her pointed use of his name—made his eyes jump from the rack of DVDs he'd been examining to hers. "A drink?"

She took in a breath and forced herself to stay calm. Justin thought she had ice surrounding her? How about Antarctica? "Yes, drink. Glass containing liquid, preferably alcoholic, intended to be consumed orally."

He chuckled and put his hands on his hips in that manly-man way he did. "I'd love a drink. Whadya got?"

"Most everything."

He narrowed his eyes, challenging. "Irish whiskey?"

"Jameson's?"

"Damn, you're good."

"Yes." She held his gaze for a sensual beat. "I am."

She knew without looking at him that his eyes followed her to the built-in cabinet that housed her meager supply of rarely touched booze. Already he'd noticed the change and was wondering what was going on.

Before she opened the cabinet, she kicked out of her

shoes and took off her black sweater, exposing a black short-sleeved top that hung just to the waistband of her black pants. The next layer would come off soon. Then the next. After that, no more layers.

"Water? Ice? Straight up?"

"Straight up."

She poured him two fingers of Jameson's and one for herself, noting with irony the company's motto, *Sine Metu,* which Justin had once explained to her meant "Without Fear."

"Cheers." She handed Denver his drink without fear, clinked with him and took a sip, enjoying the rare treat. She still liked the taste of alcohol, but no longer wanted to tangle with its effects.

"Want to sit?" She pointed to the couch and sat at one end, leaning back against the arm. "Thanks again for your help tonight."

"You're welcome. How did Natalie like her dare?"

"She...took it fine. Of course she was embarrassed. I can tell she really wants this guy she works out with. And when a woman wants a man, I think she should go after him." She tipped her head to one side and took the elastic out of her ponytail so her long hair swung free. "Don't you think?"

Again the narrow-eyed gaze. "Depends."

She straightened and made a show of tossing the hair back from her face. He was watching every move she made. Intently. She found herself both excited by what she had to do and dismayed by how it could affect their friendship. She tried as hard as she could to suppress any signs of that conflict. Keep it easy, purely sexual. She'd done that routine many times before. Too many to be proud of. "Depends on what?"

"What she's up to." He gestured slightly toward her with his drink. "And why."

Lindsay faltered for a second, then gave a careless shrug. "What she's up to is getting the guy. *Why* is obvious. She's attracted to him. Wants him. Lusts."

The tiniest compression of his lips before he spoke. "I guess it can be that simple."

But it's usually not, was the unspoken ending to his sentence and she was starting to think he wasn't talking about Natalie and her lab partner any more than she was.

"What kind of dare would you choose for me?"

He frowned, not the reaction she'd hoped for. "That's easy. I'd dare you to tell me what you're doing right now."

She gave him a sultry smile to hide her uneasiness. "Right now? Talking to you."

He didn't smile back. "Okay."

What had she expected? That a perceptive guy like Denver wouldn't think it was odd when her entire personality changed in the course of an hour?

Damn it. She wanted this whole night back to do over. She could catch her half sisters in the act of swapping dare slips and instead have been able to send Tanya home with a stomach full of butterflies over what she'd have to do the next day when her science guy showed up to work.

Still…she had to get this done. Get the seduction over with and get back to life as usual, if God would grant her that luxury after what she was about to perpetrate. "So…Denver."

"So…Lindsay."

"Don't you think it's time you and I did something…" She pulled at the hem of her shirt until it came off over her head. She made herself appear relaxed again, wearing only a black cotton camisole. "…about what's between us?"

He froze, one, two, three seconds, then his eyes wandered over her bare arms, down over her breasts, half exposed by the low thin material, and back up to her face. The tension was so thick that she shuddered when he put his drink down on her coffee table. Which left his hands free. Didn't it.

Would he take the lead now? Take her hard and fast, then say thanks, babe, it was great, and let's do it again sometime and good night?

A girl could only hope…

He didn't. He clasped his hands behind his head and leaned against the back of the couch, eyes narrowed. If this was a movie, he'd be about to say, "make my day."

"Is that a no?"

He shook his head, his gaze pinning her so that she had to force herself not to squirm guiltily. Not a no. Which meant it was a yes?

She didn't know whether she felt relief or not.

"Mmm, good." She put her hand on the iron of his thigh and started a slow path toward where it counted, getting more and more jittery when he just sat there, staring at her.

Okay. Fine. Whatever he was into, she'd make it

work. She'd probably encountered just about every kind of guy out there along the tortured, unhappy path she'd chosen to walk before Ty's death, and done just about everything there was to do at least once. He couldn't surprise her.

She let her hand linger near his fly and was rewarded with instant swelling between his legs. To her surprise, she reacted nearly as strongly, arousal starting a low burn between hers.

Down, girl. Keep it under control.

"You like this?"

"Yes." The syllable was curt; he still hadn't moved otherwise. But as long as he wasn't objecting...

"How about this?" Her palm moved over the long, narrow bulge in his jeans. She took in a sharp breath, unprepared for her own reaction, though she'd anticipated his. Stroking him gently up and down, she leaned forward, dipping one shoulder so her strap would slide off and her hair would make a solid curtain behind her profile.

His hips moved up slightly; his breathing became audible. Her arousal matched his pace, maybe because it had been a long time for her. She unsnapped his jeans, drew the zipper down more hurriedly than she'd intended, dipped her hand in to savor his warmth and his hardness through his black cotton briefs.

"Lindsay." His voice was husky.

"Mmm?" She bent down and kissed his erection, her lips lingering.

"Why are you doing this?"

She tugged his jeans down, reached for the waist-band of his briefs and pulled them down to expose him. He was beautiful. Thick and long and tipped faintly pink. Her hunger grew. "Because I want you. Haven't you figured that out yet?"

"I have figured it out. What I haven't figured out is why tonight."

"You know a better time?" She pressed her face against his length, inhaled his scent, then opened her mouth and slid it along his erection aiming for the tip to take him fully into her—

He grabbed her shoulders and had her half lying across the back of the couch under him so quickly that she couldn't control her terror reaction, and heard herself make the choked cry she hadn't had to let out in a long time.

"Where is this coming from, Lindsay?"

She swallowed the thickness in her throat, telling herself over and over that this was Denver, this was different, he was emotional not dangerous, confused not enraged until the urge to plead for mercy left her and she could feel as impassive as she was struggling to appear. "What are you talking about?"

"Months, Lindsay. Months of dancing around this, avoiding me, shutting me out, and now suddenly you're all hot to give me a blow job? What the hell happened?"

"I thought…you'd like it."

"Geezus, Lindsay. Of course I'd like it. I'm a guy. But I think we skipped a few parts of this equation. Like spending time together first—you wouldn't even come swimming with me. Like talking about something other than work. Or…" His voice dropped lower; he fixed his gaze on her mouth. "…like kissing."

No. Not kissing. Not sweetness. Not affection. No feeling. She made another desperate sound and threw herself to the opposite end of the couch, arms crossed around her chest.

"What the—" He held his hands up, surrendering.

She closed her eyes. Maybe she could have messed this up more, but she didn't think so. Why couldn't he just let her show him a good time? Why did he have to make this about anything except screwing her so she could fulfill her dare?

"I'm sorry." She sat up ramrod straight, the way she had refused to do during adolescence for her furious mom. "This was not a good idea. I knew it wasn't, but I—"

"Lindsay." His voice was slow, gentle, talking nicey-nice to the completely insane woman. She didn't blame him. "Let's get back to our whiskey. Back to talking. Back to normal. Tomorrow you can come swimming with me after work or I'll come up here again or I'll take you to lunch one day before work. Maybe a lot of days, maybe one or two late night dinners and we'll see what happens. Let this go more naturally and a lot slower."

She bit her lip. How the hell was she supposed to tell him that was the last thing she wanted to do?

Or…maybe next to last. Or maybe…

It couldn't happen. He was talking relationship and all she could handle in her life right now was sex. If it wasn't for the dare, she wouldn't even choose to handle that.

"I'm sorry, Denver. It's not like that. I was just looking to get laid and I thought you were too. You were nice enough to help me bring the boxes up here, you were looking really good, I was horny and I thought maybe you'd be up for it. But the whole sweetheart dating, kissing thing? No. Sorry. Not a good plan. Not for me."

She finished, pretty pleased with herself. Guys understood the need to get laid. He'd get it. She'd be off the hook and they could get back to—

"Why not?"

Her pleasure started to evaporate. "Why not what?"

"Why isn't the 'whole sweetheart dating, kissing thing' a good idea?"

Crap. He had that look back, the one where he thought he already knew the answer but just wanted to go through the formality of having her say it out loud. Maybe men thought acting as though they knew you better than you did was sexy. She had to mark it down as one of the most irritating characteristics they possessed.

"Because…" Her mind failed. She couldn't come up with a single reason, especially not with him sitting in her living room with his pants undone, firm skin showing at his abdomen, a slight flush to his cheeks, eyes intently dark, handsome and so damn noble. "It's not what I want."

"Ah. Okay, then." He got up abruptly and the force of the pain squeezing into her chest startled her. "It is what I want so until one of us changes his or her mind I guess this isn't going to happen, huh."

His tone was offhand, but his look said he was asking her a question, not making a statement.

"Right." She nodded, wishing he'd leave so she could throw herself onto her bed and let this new troubling misery have its way with her. What had she done here? What had she unleashed? She should have followed her instincts and refused to take a dare. Everything was going so well before this…

Still she couldn't have gone back on the dare without undermining the organization that had done so much not only to empower its members but for her as well. How else could she have met and become friendly with so many strong, interesting women? Her acquaintances prior to this had been pretty unappealing. Now she felt part of a community that had more on its mind than sex, drugs and rebellion.

More importantly, how else could she have gracefully and anonymously made contact with her half sisters? One invitation sent out to each of them last September had been the perfect way to introduce them to her, though only Katie took her up on joining at first. Bottom line, she'd had no choice but to accept the dare. Now she was paying a price. Another one.

Denver put his pants back together, drained the rest of his drink and took the glass and hers into the kitchen like the good bar manager he was.

At the door he turned, gaze probing again, asking her the question that must be going through his head. What the hell had happened to make her suddenly act the way she did? Was she that disturbed? "Good night. See you tomorrow."

"Tomorrow." Lindsay nodded and managed a smile. "Good night."

She closed the door after him. Maybe he'd give up now. Maybe he'd decide she was some kind of lunatic and give up and leave her alone.

The thought sucked her into a whirlpool of loneliness and fear. What would her life be without Denver's constant support and concern? The support and concern she regularly stepped on and rejected and only now realized how much she relied on?

She leaned back against the door and closed her eyes.

And what the hell was she going to do about the dare?

4

DENVER TOSSED BACK WHAT he knew should be his last shot of tequila. Except he knew the shot before should have definitely been the last one and the one before that certainly should have been the last one too. Hell, he shouldn't have come here in the first place. Vito's Pub, a ridiculous name if ever there was one. The kind of place that stayed open too late for pathetic drunks.

Like ohhhh, saaaay…him.

He hadn't tied one on like this since the night he broke off his engagement to Jenna. Every second of that horrible conversation would linger in his mind until the day he died—her tears, her begging, the stabbing guilt. Then her abrupt transition into rage and accusations, mostly unfounded, though a few had hit their mark. He remembered every second of his trip back to New Haven on the train, then his cab ride from the station to Naples, the Yale campus bar. After that, things got blurry fast. The next morning he'd woken up naked on the bathroom floor of his dorm with no memory of how he'd gotten there. That had seemed like a pretty good time to decide he'd done enough drinking to last him a lifetime. After that it had been no more than two drinks, no matter what, no matter where, no matter who with. Or with whom. Or who whatever.

Until tonight. See how much goodness and joy Lindsay Beckham had brought into his life? Exactly…none. Nothing but frustration, emotionally, sexually…whatever other *lys* there were that he couldn't think of right now.

No more. Enough. He was finished. Done. Operation Lindsay was terminated. She could stay icy and shut down forever. The next day he'd turn in his resignation at Chassy. And why did she call it that anyway? Screw it. Screw her. Or rather no, no screwing her.

That thought hurt too.

He was disgusted with himself for spending a whole year of sniveling after her over and over again. Please open up to me, Lindsay. Please tell me your problems. Tonight was the worst. "I can't have sex without emotion, Lindsay. Kiss me first, tell me you love me…"

That was it. He was turning into a girlie-man. No, *she* was turning him into a girlie-man. If he was going to do that, he might as well become gay so he wouldn't have to deal with women at all anymore.

Crap. He needed to go home. No, he needed a cold swim. He was losing it.

He got up unsteadily and paid for his drinks, staggered in the doorway and caught his shoulder hard on the jamb. Maybe driving wasn't a great idea. He'd leave his car here and cab it out to Brookline.

Half an hour later, he'd managed to hail a cab, remember his parents' address, pay the driver and make his way through frosty air that smelled like snow to the Robinsons, next door to the small house his parents had moved into after he left home. They'd wanted to keep a residence in Massachusetts but intended to spend most of their time traveling the world. Which they had. They'd be back in March from their year in Paris, London and Greece. By then he'd better have a plan for the rest of his life to avoid being a thirty-five-year-old man who still lived with Mommy and Daddy.

He used his key and pushed open the sliding door to the pool, stripped naked, nearly falling on his face when he tried to balance on one leg to take off his pants. Then he dove in, swam a few furious if sloppy laps, then a few more, feeling his head clearing slightly. Finally he climbed onto the raft, only slipping off once, and lay back watching the clouds overhead.

Between Lindsay's behavior tonight and the threat of parental cohabitation, he would finally get his act together, leave Chassy and do what he was meant to do in a place that would appreciate what he had to offer. Then he'd—

"Well, hello-o-o."

Adrenaline preceded his rational reaction. What the hell was Adele doing here again tonight? He'd never encountered her two nights in a row. It must be nearly two o'clock.

"Nice night for a swim."

"Yeah." He slid back into the water, annoyed. He

couldn't help it. He'd wanted to be alone to think. Or alone so he didn't have to. One of those. "Where d'you come from every night?"

"I'm in the neighborhood."

"Which house?"

"My uncle lives down the street. I'm visiting for a while." She lifted her shirt over her head, and his drunken brain registered that her bathing suit didn't look like a bathing suit. "I'm just back from a party and felt like a swim before bed. I had the cab drop me here."

She undid her jeans and stepped out of them. The bottom half of her bathing suit didn't look like a bathing suit either. "I hope you don't mind but I didn't bother getting my suit. I didn't want to wake my uncle just to get it and then wake him again when I got home after."

Her underwear was lacy, he couldn't tell what color in the dim light. Maybe black, maybe red, very skimpy. He suddenly remembered he didn't have a suit on either. Why hadn't he done as she did and kept his underwear on?

Because he didn't know she'd show up, wasn't thinking she might. So fine, he'd stay in the water where she couldn't see anything and hope she left soon. She could swim in her underwear, and he'd—

Except… He swallowed convulsively. She was taking her underwear off.

Clouds hid the moon tonight, but the lamp outside of the pool area cast enough of a gleam that he could see…well, he could see. Her breasts were large and full with small dark nipples; the hair between her legs was waxed into a tiny strip. Her shape he already knew was stunning.

She shouldn't get in the pool naked with him. He wanted to say something but he was caught in the stupid male tug-of-war between what his brain recognized as the right thing to do and what his dick did.

She climbed down into the water, step by step on the ladder, her fabulous curving ass swinging provocatively and swam toward him. He didn't resist. Not when she wrapped her legs around him, not when she gave a tiny exclamation—not of disappointment—when she realized what he didn't have on either.

Suddenly his brain shut down, his hands went to her waist, then slid up beside her breasts, which seemed to hold him in some kind of stupid enthralled enchantment. He couldn't look away, couldn't keep himself from wanting to touch. His thumbs slid over her nipples—he swore his damn thumbs were acting on their own. This wasn't him. Why wouldn't his brain work? Her head dropped back in the kind of rapture that looked really fake, like she'd watched too many porn movies.

He moved his thumbs back to her sides. His mind restarted. This wasn't real. This wouldn't be anything more than making love to a great pair of tits.

And? his dick countered. What the hell was wrong with that? Not like it hadn't been done before, even by him, not like it never would be again…

But something didn't jibe with what just happened with Lindsay. Something… Damn brain.

To hell with it.

He lifted her, brought one breast to his mouth, suckled, tasting chlorine and unfamiliar skin. The feel of her breasts was odd, which made him think she must have had them done.

More fake.

"Oh. Ohhh. *Ohhhhh.* Denver…" Her voice was low, urgent; she squeezed her legs and pressed her sex eagerly against his lower abdomen. "Do me, babe. Ple-e-ease. Now. Right here. Ohhhh, yeah."

The breathy plea was over the top. He sighed and closed his eyes in pain.

He couldn't. God damn it, but he couldn't.

"Adele." Her name came out on a groan. "Why are you doing this to me?"

"Because you are soooo hot and I'm soooo horny."

Right. He had to ask. If he was going to have meaningless sex, he might as well have it with Lindsay since that was all she wanted. He might as well take some pleasure along with the girlie-man pain she was dishing out.

"It's not…I can't…" He let out a swift breath of frustration. "It just isn't going to work."

"You said that last time." She relaxed her legs from his waist and reached down to his cock, hard as granite in the cool water, dipping her face then reappearing. "I think it's working just fine."

"Down there I'm good to go. But here…" He tapped his head, then realized what he was saying and nearly roared in exasperation. *Way to go, girlie-man.*

He shifted away and reached the ladder of the pool,

managing to get up one step, staggered back and she was there behind him, wrapping her arms around him. "Wait."

He waited—not that he could do otherwise short of dragging her over rough tile—cock still hard, her firm breasts pressing against his back not making penile deflation likely any time soon.

"It's her still? The woman from work?" Her voice was sweet and seductive. Her hands started caressing his abdomen.

"No. That's over." He didn't sound convincing even to himself.

"She's got someone else?" Her hands didn't stop roaming down from his abdomen through coarse hair stopping shy of his penis, which twitched each time in anticipation.

"She's got baggage." He spat the word out, wondering why he wasn't telling her to stop what she was doing. Maybe because it felt good. Maybe he was a manly-man after all.

"Ohhh, I'm sorry." Her fingers tickled over his thigh, made a sideways sweep to brush his balls. "So maybe she'll come around?"

"Maybe."

Her hand closed over his cock; his body tensed and she backed off, went back to stroking around him. Tease. Or was he the tease here? "Maybe she has business stuff to worry about?"

"Yeah, maybe." He swayed, arousal and confusion and alcohol making this very, very complicated. "She's trying to attract investors, to expand the place."

"Ah, that does sound complicated." Her feathery touch explored again. "You want her real bad, huh."

"Yeah." The confession came out stupidly hoarse and anguished. Where was his cool? In the bottom of the tequila bottle. Damn his dive back into that poison.

"Is she beautiful?"

"Yes." A vision of Lindsay, taking off her sweater, revealing herself to him in the black camisole filled his mind. "Very."

"Tell me about her." Her hand settled on his erection again.

He closed his eyes and pictured Lindsay, didn't resist the hand trying to drive him wild. Adele's voice coming from behind him in the darkness was like an angel's. Or a devil's. He suddenly didn't care which. "Blond. Tall. Slender. Tough."

"You can't stop wanting her even though you know you should give up."

He drew in a breath. "Yeah."

"You want her hard and fast? Or slow and sweet?"

"Both."

Her fingers circled his cock; she started an expert quick rhythm. "You want to see her blond hair spread over a mattress, don't you…"

"Yessss."

"You want to see her body emerge from her clothes, you want to taste her breasts, have her nipples between your teeth, your mouth between her legs."

"Adele." He protested even as he pumped helplessly into her skillful fingers, the picture of his tongue buried in Lindsay's sex making him insane with lust. "Why are you doing this?"

"Shhh. You want to punish her for what she's doing to you. What she's done to you. Push her down on the bed, strip her and bury yourself inside her."

He was desperately, drunkenly aroused by her words, by the picture, by the idea of finally getting to be with Lindsay in every carnal sense of the phrase.

"She'll wrap her legs around you, trying to get you in deeper. She'll pant and writhe and scratch your back and then come in a huge wave and scream your name."

He was getting close. He felt caught by the picture her words painted, as ineffectual against them as he felt around Lindsay. This was so twisted.

"Or she'll struggle and nearly escape, and you'll overwhelm her, take her from behind, in hard until she's helpless with how good it feels to have you inside her, filling her, pushing yourself against her sweet little ass…"

It was too much. Too much. He gave in, the orgasm swept him, hot and viciously satisfying.

Then he slowly came down, and awareness returned, the slight lap of the water against his thighs, the push of Adele's fake breasts against his lower back.

Oh God. What had he started? Now he needed to turn around, lift her up against him, and give her the same satisfaction she'd given him. He wasn't in high school anymore, using women for his own arrogant pleasure, then thanks, seeya, didn't cut it. He needed to even the score.

But he'd be forcing himself. He wasn't going to be

able to touch Adele with any passion or enjoyment. What the hell had he been thinking? He could be with Lindsay right now if orgasms were all he wanted.

Except they weren't. Not from her.

"Wow." His voice sounded forced. "That was…unexpected."

She laughed, a low sexy purr in her throat. "Mmm, ver-r-ry sexy."

"Yeah." He turned on the ladder, weariness and booze making his muscles heavy and stiff. He'd give anything to be able to go straight home and sleep this bizarre night off. But he had his honor.

"Come here." He sat on the edge and reached for her reluctantly.

She giggled, pushed off, swam to the middle of the pool and turned back to look at him.

Oh no. She wasn't going to make him play some cute cat and mouse game…

"Go home, Denver."

"What?" He stared in disbelief. Had he heard her correctly?

"Go home." She made shooing motions with her hands that splashed the water up around her.

"You don't want me to—" He made a half-hearted gesture toward her.

"No. I milked all the energy out of you. And frankly, I'm not wild about being with a guy who just came thinking of someone else."

Uh. Twisted logic, but logic of some kind. He wasn't one to talk tonight about making sense.

"Right." He gripped the pool's edge, hunched his shoulders and moved his lower legs in the water. "You surprised me."

"My gift to you. Now go."

This was odd. Why wouldn't she want what she'd given out? "You're sure?"

"Yes." Her voice held amused exasperation. "More than sure, go!"

He waited a beat, then got up and squinted at her, treading water in the middle of the pool. Something wasn't quite right about all this but he was too tired and too full of Lindsay and tequila to make sense of anything.

He pulled on his clothes, let himself out with a final wave, then trudged through the cold, bitter against his damp skin. The first flakes of snow were falling, slowly, innocently, onto his hot aching head. February might mean spring in some states but Massachusetts still clung tightly to winter.

At his parents' house, he drank as much water as his stomach could hold to ward off the worst of the hangover he'd undoubtedly suffer. Then he fell on the mattress, temples throbbing, stomach rumbling ominously.

Tomorrow he was going to feel like crap, not that he didn't thoroughly deserve to on a lot of fronts. He just wasn't sure right now which would be worse, the upset in his body or what he already carried in his heart.

"Hey, hi, hello." Joey barged into Lindsay's office, making Lindsay mess up her signature on a check to the utility company and launching her into full-scale jitters instead of only half-scale. Denver wasn't due for another three hours but she was edgy after their disastrous escapade last night. How would he act today? After the inevitable awkward first moments would they go back to their relationship as it used to be? Or had she ruined their friendship over a stupid party game?

Add to that, she wasn't interested in the coming inquisition, which could be the only reason Joey had shown up at the bar at lunchtime.

"And?"

Lindsay took her time stuffing the check into the return envelope and turned slowly, reacting as if she were just now registering Joey was there. "Why hello, sister dear. How did you sleep last night after all those Valentinis? What a lovely suit! Blue is so your color. And is that a new briefcase?"

Joey set the briefcase down and folded her arms across her chest with a look of disapproval. Clearly Lindsay's sarcasm had rolled right off. "*And?* How was last—"

"What are you doing here so far afield, Ms. Winfield? Shouldn't you be in court litigating someone's pants off? Or at home doing the literal same to Sebastian?"

"You're stalling."

"Avoiding."

"Now you're hair-splitting." Joey's blue gaze turned persuasive. "C'mon, you have to tell."

"Ooh, well, guess what…" Lindsay leaned forward, beckoning as if she were about to spill the whole delicious story. "No, I don't."

Joey studied Lindsay so closely Lindsay had to fight not to drop her gaze. "Oh my God."

"What now?" Lindsay tried not to sound defensive and annoyed but didn't have much luck.

"You didn't sleep with him, did you?"

Busted. Lindsay plunked the sealed envelope in the *paid* pile, grabbed up a folder and went swiftly to her file cabinet, apparently her favorite spot for looking busy when she was flustered. "You can think what you want."

"What happened?" Her voice softened into concern. "Did you lose your nerve?"

"Please." Lindsay sent Joey a scornful look, as if she'd been cool as a cucumber over the entire concept.

"So what, then? He lost his?"

Lindsay shrugged. The easy intimacy her half sisters enjoyed and expected from her, was still such a struggle. "Something like that."

"Oh, no, Lindsay." Joey laid a sympathetic hand on her arm, then withdrew it when Lindsay flinched. "So he wouldn't…"

"No." Granted, he'd turned her down because he wanted more than sex or said he did, but she didn't owe Joey that much. And Joey wouldn't know what to make of it, anyway. What man would turn down a willing woman he was clearly attracted to? Certainly none of the men the Winfield sisters had offered themselves to on their Martini Dares. Liam, David and Sebastian had been right there, making sure a lot more than just the dare was wholly and perfectly fulfilled.

"Hmm." Joey frowned and tapped her finger against

pursed lips. "That makes no sense. Last night he was looking at you as if he wanted to eat you whole."

"Apparently he doesn't."

"Come on, it was obvious to everyone."

"Joey, I was there. He didn't want to."

"Right. Okay. Sorry. But men don't look at women like that just for fun. And they're not bright enough to fake it." She drew a chair away from the wall, sat and folded her hands like a general about to develop a battle plan. "So."

"So?"

"When are you going to try again?"

Lindsay knew that was coming. And knew just as surely that her answer wouldn't be accepted. "I thought probably next never."

"You know it's funny." Joey leaned back, looking off into the distance. "I seem to recall a certain incident involving someone named Joey who wasn't allowed to rest by a certain trio, named Brooke, Katie and Lindsay until her darkest secret was revealed to the man of her dreams, and her dare therefore completed. Ring any bells?"

"You and Sebastian were meant to be together in a relationship so it was worth it. Maybe Denver and I just aren't." She tried to shrug carelessly but the catch in her voice gave her away. Damn it.

"Oh, right, obviously. Because the first time you tried to jump his bones it was completely out of the blue and he wasn't prepared. He probably wanted to know what the hell was going on instead of just jumping on whatever female part was available. Obviously you couldn't tell him it was a dare so he'd be even more confused when you couldn't explain and that proves that he's not right for you...how?"

Rule one: Never argue with a lawyer.

Lindsay swallowed hard. Joey had come uncomfortably close to the truth. Most of the previous night, Lindsay had gone over this and over this, concluding that the only way she was going to save her sanity was to tell herself sex with Denver simply wasn't going to happen on his terms since he made it clear it wouldn't happen on hers. Therefore she could put the whole idea to rest and move on with what she needed to accomplish. By dawn she'd convinced herself her half sisters would understand if he'd rejected her and that this good and rational argument would win the day.

Right now things weren't looking that simple. "Joey, you're—"

"He needs time to adjust. I guarantee he spent the night thinking about you." Joey winked slyly. "Probably had to have some...you know...intimate time with himself because of it. This morning he'll be all over you. Trust me on this."

Lindsay made an exasperated noise, unable to stop the stupid leap of her heart. "I really don't want to keep you, Dr. Joey, office therapist. I'm sure you have other patients to visit. So by all means—"

"What's so funny, Joey? Hi, Lindsay." Katie burst into the office, fair skin flushed from the cold, blond curling hair tousled into a lovely mess by the wind. "So? What'd I miss? How'd it go last night?"

Lindsay threw up her hands and let them smack

down on her thighs. "Excuse me, do either of you have the slightest awareness that you're intruding on my time, my job and most especially my personal life?"

"Sure." Katie blinked innocently. "Doesn't bother me though. You, Joey?"

"Hmm." Joey shook her head. "I'd have to say... Nope."

"So? What went on?" Katie glanced first at Lindsay, then obviously saw how far that would get her and turned expectantly to her older sister.

Joey shook her head mournfully.

"Oh no." Katie's eager look dimmed. "Bad?"

"The boy wouldn't bite. Or nibble. Or suck."

"Aw, bummer." Katie looked dismayed, then brightened. "So when's she going to try again?"

"Excuse me." Lindsay signaled a time-out, hands in a *T* formation. "Do *I* have any say in this?"

"No." Both women spoke together in that refined Winfield way that allowed no argument.

Lindsay put her head in her hands and let herself crack up. It was either that or scream. She had certainly met her match in the Stubborn Infuriating Department with her half sisters. "Where's Brooke? I'm surprised she's not here with a tape recorder to find out exactly what went on."

"Oh, she'll be here soon," Katie said happily.

"Who'll be here soon?"

Lindsay lifted her head to see, who else, Brooke striding in, grinning at her sisters, snowflake glitter from one of her department store window displays caught in her rich brown hair.

"Is there *no* such thing as privacy anymore?"

"Huh?" Brooke clapped a hand to her chest, the picture of offended innocence. "I don't know about these gossipy vultures who undoubtedly have the full scoop and will share very soon or else, but *I*, the always tactful and caring older sibling, am just here to deliver invites to the annual Winfield Valentine's Day party."

Joey and Katie coughed loudly. Brooke shot them a smug grin and handed Lindsay a heavy cream envelope. "You haven't made it to any of the family's monthly dinners but we'd really like you to come to this one, Lindsay. Like it or not, you're one of us now, and Valentine's Day is a special time for the Winfields, the day Grandpa Henry and Grandma Evelyn got married."

Flustered, Lindsay opened the envelope and peeked inside. She might be related but she'd never be one of them. "*Engraved* invitations to a family dinner?"

"This would be more of a formal ball," Joey said cheerfully. "Nowadays it's just family and hangers-on. In the old days, Grandpa Henry and Grandma Evelyn used to invite hundreds, the cream of Boston society."

"So why am *I* invited?"

Katie rolled her eyes. "Cut the Lil Orphan Annie stuff. You're family and we'd like you with us to celebrate."

"Thank you." Lindsay closed the envelope again, touched, but resolute. She'd rather stick pins in her eyes than show up at some overly formal occasion where she could feel even more out of place than she did already. She already pictured this Grandpa Henry—the admiral—tall, white-haired, scowling in a military uniform he never took off with his nose pointed permanently skyward.

"And bring Denver." Katie winked.

"Speaking of which…" Joey waggled her finger in Lindsay's direction. "Another try tonight."

"Uh-oh. *Another* try?" Brooke watched Lindsay, her forehead wrinkled in concern. "The first one didn't take?"

"Nope." Joey shook her head. "I think it was probably too sudden for him."

"She needs to e-e-ease him into the idea." Katie accompanied her words with a raunchy visual aid.

"Good plan." Brooke nodded, rolling her eyes at her snickering sisters. "Flirt with him today and he'll go for it tonight for sure. Holding back is proof he's a nice guy too. Most of them jump on whatever's put out for the taking. Like three men we've been recently acquainted with, ahem."

Katie giggled; Joey waggled her eyebrows lasciviously.

Lindsay couldn't help smiling even though her insides were knotted with dread. Whenever she tried out protests in her head, she'd flash back to a time when one of the sisters or another Martinis and Bikinis member was making the same arguments against completing her own dare. Lindsay had never softened. Too bad she didn't have a time machine handy to go back and change that.

Except if she had relented, her half sisters might not have gotten together with Liam, David and Sebastian, the loves of their lives. The three sisters would argue that Denver was undoubtedly hers. But you didn't have to look far to see the differences between how Winfield lives worked out and how Lindsay's did. "Look, girls, I—"

"If at first you don't succeed…"

"Forget that stuff." Joey waved Brooke's encouragement away. "It's the rules. You're a member. You have to follow them. Period."

"Like we all did," Katie said.

"I can't." The words slipped out automatically. Though she believed the battle was lost, the stupid eternally hopeful part of her that somehow had survived her mess of an upbringing, seeing the happiness in her half sisters' eyes, was foolish enough to want what they had, what she'd always longed for—the kind of perfect love that healed and brought soul-lifting joy.

Even after her pursuit in all the wrong places brought only more hurt, she'd never been able to abandon that dream completely. She'd just pushed it as far away as she could. Until now. Until meeting Denver, discovering her half sisters and drawing her first Martini Dare.

"Why can't you?" Her half sisters spoke all at once; none of whose faces looked ready to give her objection the slightest bit of weight.

"Because I…because he…" *Wants more than I can give him.* She couldn't say that. The obvious response from her half sisters would be again, *Why? Why can't you give him more?*

And she wasn't sure she had a better answer than *fear.*

5

BY THE TIME DENVER WAS DUE in to work at three-thirty, Lindsay had managed to convince herself that everything would soon be back to normal between them. He'd roll with the punches and she'd give no sign that anything had changed. If she ever did try the dare again, it would be under vastly different circumstances. For sure not tonight. She needed some time to detox and make sure their friendship had stabilized.

Unless of course her half sisters were right and Denver had spent his night as restless and sexually tormented as she had. Unless he showed up having decided to hell with relationship issues, he wanted her as much as she wanted him and they were going to party naked all night.

The thought thrilled her more than thoughts should. She'd learned to trust only what was right in front of her face. Thinking led only to fantasy, and fantasy led straight to a big list of what you didn't have. Or couldn't have. At least in Lindsay's case. Her half sisters could probably fulfill every fantasy within the hour, even those that—

"Hi, Lindsay."

His voice was deeper than usual, and cooler. She turned, making sure she didn't look anxious or eager. "Hi, Denver."

"Everything okay?"

"I'm fine."

"I meant the bar."

"Oh." Her stomach twisted. She nodded too many times. Way too many times. Didn't sound as if he'd changed his mind about last night at all. "Right. Yes, everything's fine. We're covered. Should be a good crowd tonight, Friday."

He hesitated, and she was suddenly terrified he'd walk out without saying anything else. "And…are you okay?"

"Sure." More nodding. Imbecilic nodding as relief swept over her. He'd asked. They were on their way back to normal after all. "You?"

"Sure."

She was skeptical. He didn't look okay. He sounded croaky and looked exhausted and puffy around the eyes. So he was giving her a taste of her own medicine by withholding his real emotional state—a fairly unpleasant glimpse into what she put him through nearly every day.

"Well. Good."

The silence stretched until her relief ran whimpering away. The awkwardness between them was nearly unbearable and he wasn't rushing to fix it. Her resolve to act as if nothing happened dissolved. Still she didn't know what to do instead.

For God's sake, Lindsay, say something. Apologize.

Do something. She couldn't. The fear was too strong. That he'd reject her. That he was still angry and would become angrier if she mentioned what had happened last night again.

"So…if you need me, I'm going to take inventory."

"Okay," she said too brightly. "Thanks."

He nodded and disappeared into the bar.

Her face burning, Lindsay sank into her desk chair. *Good job, Lindsay.* She'd screwed everything up. Everything. Gone against her instincts, tried to do the stupid dare, then lied to him that she only wanted to get laid, pretending he meant nothing more to her than that. Now she was reaping her just reward.

The sudden emotional pain was so fierce, she leapt up from her chair. Activity. That was what she needed. Work always saved her from herself. She sure as hell could have used that knowledge in her teens and twenties. Better late than never.

She queued the evening's music, mended a few Valentine decorations, replacing a few that had gotten mangled. When the postwork crowd arrived, she helped fill in for the missing waitress, running drinks and appetizers, clearing plates and glasses and finally concluded that in this case, activity didn't do squat.

Denver was avoiding her. Avoiding her looks, avoiding her smiles, and as much as she went through the motions of chatting and laughing with the customers, the depression threatening to overwhelm her pointed to one blindingly obvious conclusion: she wasn't quite the untouchable island she thought she'd become.

So the question was, did she refortify herself? Or further strip her defenses? Strengthening her defenses was more familiar and safer, but the opposite… She glanced at Denver behind the bar, grinning at a patron leaning toward him in a low-cut shirt.

Well, she'd think about it.

By eleven forty-five, the crowd had thinned in preparation for midnight closing, and Lindsay went into her office to calculate and distribute tips from credit card payments. When the phone rang, she reached for it absently, engrossed in computations.

"Hey, there, Lindsay."

Gina's low, throaty voice usually made Lindsay's gut sink. This time it was already so low she barely reacted. Fitting that Gina would call tonight. "What do you want?"

"How's February treating you?"

"Not too well, actually." She closed her eyes wearily. Like she'd admit the bar had been packed most nights and she was doing fine?

"Hmm, that's not what I hear."

"No?" *From whom?* A spying customer? She wanted to lay her head on the desk and scream. "What do you hear?"

"Enough to think I could ask my old friend and boss for a raise."

No. *No.* It was enough what Lindsay was paying. Much more and she'd risk presenting to potential investors financial records that weren't as healthy as they should be, that might raise red flags. "You don't need a raise, Gina. You get more than many people on the planet make in a lifetime."

"Oh, yes. So true… You know, the other day I was remembering something."

Lindsay had to loosen her grip on the receiver. She was pressing it so tightly against her ear that her temple ached. "I don't want to know."

"I was thinking how Ty's last words were how much he loved you. And how he wanted to keep you with him for the rest of his life." She gave a sigh as if the twisted taunts Ty had thrown at Lindsay had been words of touching devotion. "Right before you pushed him down the stairs."

Lindsay closed her eyes. That was exactly how Gina would paint the incident to a jury. Lindsay could say that Ty had been giving the words an entirely different, threatening meaning, but she couldn't deny that he'd said them. And who would believe the story of a woman motivated by escaping jail time over the testimony of a woman with nothing at stake who'd promised to tell the whole truth and nothing but?

"How much?"

"We can talk details another time, hon. I know you must be busy right now. What else is going on? Anything new in your love life?"

Lindsay's eyes shot open. Why would Gina ask that? Especially now? Even more especially in that smarmy knowing tone? "Nothing."

"Pity. I have a little something starting up with a totally sexy guy."

How nice for her.

A tap on her door, then Denver's voice. "Lindsay?"

Immediately Lindsay rose in panic and dropped her voice. "I have to go."

"I'll tell you about him another time then. He is supremely hot. Probably just your type too."

"Sure, okay, bye." She jammed down the phone and took a few seconds to breathe, hoping she could hide her emotions. At that moment she felt as if she were trying to conceal Niagara Falls behind a hankie. "Hi, Denver. What's going on?"

He glanced at her face, did a double take, then looked back down at the glass he was wiping dry; he must be helping Justin behind the bar tonight. "Ralph Gebring wants to talk to you. As usual."

"Right. Sure. Okay." She nodded—again—and got up, smiling determinedly. Denver hadn't asked her what was wrong. She never put much stock in the saying that you didn't know what you had until it was gone because she hadn't ever lost anything she missed. Until now.

"Table six."

"Thanks." Her voice broke.

She needed to get out of here before she fell apart in front of him. As much as it hurt she deserved his treatment; she knew that. She'd rejected him at every turn. How could she expect that he'd keep coming around no matter how often and how hard she kept kicking him away?

She had anyway.

"I'll talk to him." She took two steps then realized

she'd have to brush past Denver in the doorway. "After you."

He stayed where he was, watching her with dark, moody eyes. The tension between them was so palpable she could barely breathe. What was he thinking?

At the exact second she was going to start ripping her hair out, he stepped aside.

She fled, not sure she could stand a whole lot more of this. What had he wanted standing there staring at her? Why hadn't he told her? Why hadn't he said something?

Why hadn't she?

She reached table six and put on a polite face for rotund, greasy-haired, vaguely lecherous Ralph Gebring, who she had to be nice to because his wealthy Aunt Marie was her best candidate for investing in the bar expansion. Lindsay had avoided commercial and government lending institutions so far, afraid they'd have the resources to dig too deeply and unearth her past.

When she first took over Chassy, she'd made minor cosmetic changes. But now her dream included taking over the Yarn Barn next door which would be up for sale in March when the owner retired, adding a room for dancing and live music, more tables in the main room and an expanded, upgraded menu.

Ralph came in every week and seemed to think talking to Chassy's owner gave him some kind of cachet. Generally he summoned her right before closing when he was at his loosest and most dull.

Ten endless minutes later, she excused herself in the middle of an overly detailed recitation of his family's vacation and went over to the large central bar decorated with her paper Valentines and blinking miniature hearts. She didn't think she'd ever been so ready to have a business day behind her.

"Quitting time, Justin."

"Righty-oh, mighty Lindsay."

She growled only half-jokingly and returned to her office. The phone rang again and she gave it a look of intense hatred before picking it up, daring it to be Gina again.

"Lindsay, it's Brooke."

She closed her eyes, first in relief, then in irritation when she realized Brooke would be calling to give her some rah-rah speech about seducing Denver again. "Look. I am not going to do the dare. I damaged my friendship with him, I made a fool out of myself and I can't deal with you all harassing me into—"

"Lindsay."

She took a deep breath. "What?"

"I called because I was a little worried about you. Now I'm a lot worried about you."

"I'm fine." The response was automatic and she wasn't surprised by Brooke's snort of disbelief.

"Oh. Yeah. You sound really fine. Happy enough to put clams to shame."

Her lips curved grudgingly. Despite sometimes wanting to throttle her new family, the Winfield sisters could almost always get her smiling. "That's me."

"Well…since you brought it up, I've been thinking about your approach to Denver."

Lindsay sighed. "Do we have to—"

"Yup," Brooke said brightly. "I was thinking you should try being more direct."

"More direct than throwing myself at him?"

"No. More honest. Tell him about the meeting and how we turned the tables on you and your plan for Tanya. Tell him Martini Dares are about forcing yourself to do something you want to do deep down but haven't found the nerve. Tell him your sisters pushed you in the right direction but maybe in the wrong vehicle."

Lindsay swallowed, trying to get the tension out of her throat.

"Does that make sense?" Her half sister's voice was unbearably gentle. "It would kill two birds—repair the damage and let you complete your dare once he understood where the change of heart was coming from."

"Right." Except it wasn't that simple. Her half sisters didn't know about his ultimatum that sex between them had to mean more than getting each other off.

"But, Lindsay…" Brooke's tone changed, becoming so serious Lindsay immediately braced for teasing. "The plan would entail doing this thing humans do called ar-tic-u-lat-ing your feel-ings."

Lindsay snorted. Touché. "Yeah, I got that part."

"Obviously I don't know him well but he seems like the kind of guy who wouldn't mind. Might welcome it even. There are some men—not many, that's for sure— who can actually handle women sharing their feelings." A male protest sounded faintly in the background, undoubtedly David, Brooke's hunky baseball star boyfriend. "I bet Denver is one of the very, *very* few, who—"

A squeal, then words muffled by her hand over the receiver. Another squeal, then a laugh.

Lindsay found herself grinning, happy for Brooke and envious as well. Apparently David was exacting delicious revenge for the male bashing. Time to bow out of the conversation. "I have to go, Brooke. Closing time."

"Right." She smothered another laugh and hushed David. "Will you think about what I said?"

"I will." Someday. Tonight she just wanted to go upstairs and sleep for a million years.

"Promise?"

"Yes. I promise. And…thanks." The word came out stiffly and she hung up, annoyed at herself. She was grateful to her half sister. Yet she couldn't even manage to express it as warmly as she felt it. Whether or not she took the advice, Brooke was sweet to worry. After a lifetime of Lindsay handling—and causing—her troubles on her own, friends like Brooke and Denver posed a new, seductive danger to her philosophy that she could only count on herself in this world.

Justin and Margaret called out good-night; she heard their voices receding, then the clink and latch of the front door. Then silence. Had Denver left without checking in or saying goodbye?

Ouch.

Had he gone swimming? He'd said he would invite her every night till she gave in…

Double ouch.

Why hadn't she ever thought she could go? Her refusal seemed so silly and churlish now.

Feeling leaden, she did the final check on the bar, locked up, turned out the lights and trudged upstairs. She could hear her mattress calling frantically.

Up in her apartment, she didn't even bother turning on the lights, heading straight for the shower. Then she fell into bed so tired she couldn't be bothered to eat anything, though her stomach felt cavernous.

Half an hour later, she was still awake, staring at the thin stripes of light coming through the blinds. Brooke was right. She didn't owe Denver her life story and every detail of her every thought. But he was important enough to her—their friendship was important enough to her—that she at least owed him a more honest explanation of what had happened the night before. It might make things better.

It couldn't make them much worse.

She got out of bed and fumbled for her cell in her pants pocket, dialed Denver's number and immediately started to panic. What would she say? What if he was swimming and she had to leave a message? She hadn't planned one. She'd just have to mumble some—

"Hi, Lindsay."

Oh God. She closed her eyes, her whole body responding to the sound of his rich somber voice. "Hi."

"What's up? Where are you?"

"In my bedr—apartment. I…need to talk to you. I mean. At some point. Now if you're not busy. Or—"

His dry chuckle mercifully cut her babble short. "I'm standing on Beaumont Street looking up at your windows wondering whether to ring the bell since it's dark and I assumed you're asleep."

"Oh." She sounded like a breathless Pollyanna. She felt like one too even though her voice remained flat and cautious. "I'm not asleep."

"Can I come up?"

"Yeah." Lindsay was already moving to the buzzer. "Come on in."

She buzzed the door open, then remembered she was wearing flowered flannel pajamas, no makeup and no restraint on her limply hanging hair.

Maybe it was just as well to look dowdy. Looking seductive had been a disaster the night before.

His steps sounded coming up to the second floor and she opened her front door, trying not to look as self-conscious as she felt. This was good. She'd at least be able to clear the air between them tonight so she could sleep.

Except he was on the last step looking at her with such intensity that she moved back, becoming wide awake. She moved back again as he came into her apartment and closed the door behind him without taking his eyes from hers. But he didn't look concerned or tender or friendly or…anything familiar.

"Hi, Denver." She had to clear her throat and focus on his chin to be able to continue. "I'm glad you're here because I wanted to talk."

"About?"

"What happened. Last night."

"Okay." He put his hands on his hips. "Talk."

This cold, rigid Denver was new to her. "We should go in the living room."

"Here is fine."

Crap. He wasn't here to reconcile. This was going to make her confession so much harder. But Brooke was right. She owed him more than the lies she'd told him about suddenly needing him for sex.

"Last night…" How the hell was she going to go about this? *Just blunder on, baby.* "…was my Martini Dare."

He narrowed his eyes in disbelief. "Your dare?"

Crap. *Crap.* This would not make things better. Instinct told her to retreat but she'd already crossed the point of no return. And she did need to make him understand even if he wouldn't forgive.

"It was supposed to be Tanya's dare night. And then, but then… Are you sure you don't want to go in the living room?"

"I can hear just as well here."

"Right." This was agony. "My sisters switched the dares and made me pick instead. And I picked one that said I had to seduce…"

She closed her eyes, jaw trembling with how much she didn't want to go on.

"I get it." He was furious. She could tell even without seeing his face. "And being a good, loyal member you lured me up here and said okay, let's go? Without thinking about how I might feel or what I might want?"

"Well…but the way you put it, it sounds—"

"Is that right? Or not?" His voice was still flat.

"That's right." She swallowed hard. His anger felt terrifyingly familiar and she'd shifted instinctively into meekness nearly calling him *sir* the way Ty used to demand,

He twisted away toward the door, stood for a moment, then slammed his palm against it with a shocking power that made her yell, reminding her again of Ty way too much.

"Don't do that."

"Damn it. Lindsay. You make me crazy. I don't even know why the hell I came up here."

"I'm sorry." Her voice came out a pathetic broken whisper. The apology was instinctive, her only defense though with Ty it stopped working eventually. "I should have told you the truth last night."

"Yes. You should have. Congratulations, you've done it. I'm sure you feel a whole lot better and good for you. I gotta go."

"Wait." He couldn't leave like this. Not until she made it right.

"For what." He turned only his head. "Not ready to let me go yet? Was this some other tactic to try and get me in the sack so you can go back to your girlfriends and brag that you bagged me?"

She shook her head, squeezed her eyes tightly shut again. Tears were close and she was starting to get desperate not to fall apart. Falling apart meant weakness, which turned on the desperation to keep the man in her life from disapproving of anything she did.

Disapproval inevitably turned to violence and violence meant pain.

Being once again in the grips of that familiar panic scared her more than Denver did. And that made her fear recede and anger take its place. Lindsay had left that meek, frightened woman far behind and no amount of male temper or macho posturing would bring her back.

She opened her eyes, met his dark accusing ones squarely. "My sisters were trying to help."

"Help? Help what?"

"Help me to get…" *Closer to you.* She couldn't go on. Couldn't make herself so vulnerable when he was like this.

"Help you to get laid?"

Her desire to make him understand vanished in a wave of rage. How dare he make condescending assumptions about what her half sisters and her club were about?

"Yes. Exactly. Help me get laid. That's their job. My personal screw associates. I just put out the call and say, 'Hey, babes, it's been a while,' and they come through for me with whatever piece of male meat looks easiest to score."

He swore and stepped forward. She stood, rock still, bracing herself. She wouldn't cry or scream.

His arms were strong…strong but not violent. His fingers tangled in her hair, turned her face up to his…forceful not cruel. "What do you get out of all this besides sex? The thrill of having brought a man to his knees?"

Lindsay stared right up into his eyes as she fought

to control her breathing—but no panic, not with him. Only clean, uncomplicated fury. "That's it. A man on his knees. That's everything I'm about. And while he's down there, his tongue better be busy."

"So that's what you want from me. Orgasms."

"Not even." She panted the words. "I can give myself those."

"Oh, right. I forgot. You're completely self-sufficient." His fingers tightened in her hair; she didn't flinch. "It must have been galling to choose a dare that meant you'd actually have to connect with another human."

She hissed between her teeth and jerked back, but he only loosened his hold, didn't let go. "I didn't even want to do the damn dare in the first place."

"Then why did you?" He pulled her back closer until their bodies were so close she could feel his warmth and his breath on her lips. In spite of her rage, she could barely control her craving for him. "Why do you let those women control you?"

"No one controls me." The comment was reflexive. No one had since Ty. Back then letting him take her over completely had felt safe. Safe! The irony made her sick now.

"Of course. My mistake. No one controls you. No one can touch you." He let his head drop back, laughed bitterly. "My life would be so much easier if I hadn't met you, Lindsay. You know that?"

Lindsay flinched. Denver wouldn't hit her but just then he might as well have. "Your life has always been easy. And you're absolutely free to walk out of mine."

He raised his head, skewered her with his gaze, angrier than she'd ever seen him. He slid his hands down, stopped them right above her ass and pulled her pelvis into contact with his. "I'm contemplating something drastic right now but that's not it."

She opened her mouth. Nothing came out. She was caught, staring into his face, feeling hers flush with a hot rush of desire.

"Screw it." She spoke suddenly and sharply, startling him. "Screw Martinis and Bikinis, screw the dare and most of all…"

His arms gripped her harder, his eyes turning darker than she'd ever seen them. "What?"

She thrust her face boldly toward his, felt his body tense, stopped a fraction of an inch from his lips and whispered her challenge. "Screw me."

6

DENVER LET GO OF HER, GRABBED her hand and pulled her after him, guessing correctly which door led to her bedroom. He wasn't going to stop and think. He was too angry, too hurt and a voice told him if he stopped to think, he was going to turn back into a girlie-man, and do something he'd regret like make himself even more vulnerable to her. Or worse, stalk away and wonder for the rest of his life what would have happened if he'd stayed.

So he'd take her up on her crude and wildly exciting offer. She armored herself every day—he would too for the time it took to satisfy them both. And if she decided tomorrow that she wanted to brag to all her friends how she'd completed her dare, then okay. He'd give her plenty to brag about.

He swung her around in the bedroom, dimly lit by one rose-shaded lamp next to her bed, put his thigh between hers, cupped her ass with both hands and rocked them together, watching for her reaction.

She shook her hair back and looked up with her trademark impassive expression, which made him even angrier. He was going to make her come so hard and so long that she'd crack that mask and show what she was feeling in her body, if not in her heart.

Instead of kissing her as he longed to, he bent his head and nipped the warm white skin of her neck. Her pulse beat fast; her breath came high; her hips pushed forward against his thigh.

Some things she couldn't control. Her body betrayed her. She was nearly as turned-on as he was.

The realization pushed his arousal higher; he made a guttural sound and practically flung her onto the bed. She fell back, watching him, her beautiful blue eyes unable to hide all the anticipation…or the trace of fear.

Tough. She was getting what she asked for. The sooner the better before one of them changed his or her mind.

He shoved down his black work pants, remembered to rescue a condom from his wallet, then freed his erection from his briefs, kicked them off and leaned forward to slide her pajama bottoms down.

She lifted to help and they came off easily, exposing her flat stomach, the widening curve of her hips, then the slightly curling hair, small pink lips protruding. He nearly spilled right there. She was perfect.

Pajamas tossed over his shoulder, he dove forward, face between her legs, heard her quick intake of breath. He stopped an inch from heaven and looked up at her with a wicked smile. She was staring at the ceiling, her small perfect breasts rising and falling with each breath, her hips raised slightly toward his mouth.

Slowly he lowered his face sensing her muscles tense

in response. He pressed a gentle, lingering kiss to her sex, then another. Then drew back and watched her again. Her eyes had closed; her lips parted; she drew her bottom lip between her teeth. Perversely, he allowed himself to enjoy her frustration. Let her be the one wanting more for a change.

Except that he wanted to taste her so badly, make her writhe, make her come that he wasn't going to be able to wait much longer. He lowered his head and thrust his tongue into her, registering her gasp with acute pleasure. He sucked hungrily, explored greedily, then settled on her clit until her long strong legs started trembling on either side of his head. She moaned and yanked her hands down to clutch the bedcovers, bracing herself for her climax.

He'd never seen anything as sexy in his life. His heart swelled dangerously, possessive thoughts intruding where they had no business.

Her breathing changed; her muscles strained to come. He raised up, sheathed himself with the condom and spread her legs with more force than he needed, knelt between them, keeping her thighs wide open with his. Then he paused and watched her watch him—but not to torture her this time. He needed to think about saving himself from torture.

If he lay on top of her, made love to her face-to-face, he'd be lost. He'd want to kiss her, gather her to him, make their physical connection an emotional one too, the rhythm slow and sweet…and leave himself wide open to her next rejection.

This was her dare. He was her toy. Last night and

again tonight. Screw me didn't mean the same as make love to me tonight and tomorrow and every tomorrow after that we have together.

He needed to hang on to his anger if he was going to get through this unscathed.

"Turn over."

Her eyes widened, then she obeyed without hesitation—she'd been as afraid of intimacy as he was but for opposite reasons—stuffing a pillow under her belly, raising her beautiful round backside toward him. He grabbed her, fortified himself with a breath, then guided his erection to her sex, hit the entrance, heard her gasp as her lips spread to welcome him. He pushed in, teeth clenched, watching his cock disappearing slowly into her tight hold, arousal kicking wildly higher.

Lindsay.

He forced the tenderness from his heart and shoved in all the way so her sex grabbed his entire length and didn't let go.

Lindsay.

He started to move, in and out, closing his eyes to concentrate on the sensation, on the sex act, on the hot pumping rhythm. Not on the woman.

Ten seconds, and his wish for blind detachment dissolved. This was Lindsay. They were together the way he'd fantasized about for months.

He slowed his pace, opened his eyes and allowed himself at least to watch her, wanting to speak but not daring to violate the anonymity further. So he screwed her with his body and made love to her in his mind. And he watched. Watched her head thrash up, then down, then to one side and then the other as her excitement grew. He traced the line of her vertebrae, paused on a tiny freckle at the small of her back, stroked the smooth skin at the base of her spine, sloped down with the gentle rounding of her backside.

She was too far away. He leaned forward, pulled her up with him. She steadied herself on one hand, back arching to keep him inside. He stroked up under her pajama top, wanting every part of her body to belong to him, her abdomen, her stomach, relishing the soft feel of her skin, and up over the small swells of her breasts, circling and rolling her nipples, responding to her intakes of breath as cues to how she liked being touched.

"Denver."

His name, said in that helpless plea of emotional desire, pierced him. There was no way this was only about the dare. He slid his hand down between her legs and found her clit and played there. She responded with a cry that shot him so near to orgasm he forced himself to slow down even more. In…then out…then in…rubbing, coaxing, teasing her, responding to her quickening jerky breaths until she gave a soft, surprised *oh* that built to a long moan. He had to grab her hips with his free hand and bury himself deep or be expelled by the force of her contractions and the tension in her trembling body.

His heart nearly burst out of his chest. *Lindsay.*

He'd intended to have her come down slowly, to prolong the lovemaking and build her up to a second orgasm.

No way. After watching her come, he was helpless to do anything but push to a rapid climax himself, a climax that nearly tore him apart.

In many more ways than one.

LINDSAY LAY ON THE BED, limp and exhausted, her body still glowing from the orgasm that had practically shot her to Mars.

So. She'd done it. Seduced Denver. She was officially off the hook for the dare. Big relief.

Except it wasn't.

The bed shifted as Denver returned, having disposed of his condom. He lay behind her, drawing her close to spoon with his large warm body.

As much as she'd tried to concentrate on the physical, on the warm skill of Denver's hands, the erotic joining of their bodies, she hadn't been able to forget they were *his* hands, and *their* bodies causing a dangerous weakness in her heart, a longing to turn over and make the act a lot more personal than it should be.

Which was bad. Because…

His hand started stroking her hair, then his fingers tangled in deeper to massage her scalp. She moaned at the delicious feeling.

Because why? Hadn't she just told herself she was safe with Denver? Didn't she understand deep down that he wasn't Ty, that he was trustworthy and kind. And now she could add incredible between the sheets.

Yes. But he was still a man and men had always treated Lindsay badly. They took over or they left. The wall she'd built up so carefully over the years wasn't going to come down with a big crash just by wanting it to. Only bit by bit, if nothing happened to shatter her faith in him.

Was that what she wanted? To slowly melt until she was open to him, totally vulnerable, maybe even truly in love?

Yes.

No.

"So now you've completed your dare." His voice was gentler but she heard what he was asking. "Congratulations."

"Yeah, thanks. I really scored." Lindsay nudged him to show she was teasing. He nudged her back, obviously getting it. Not surprisingly he had her number again.

She owed him more than a joke. But what could she say until she knew what she wanted? At this rate she'd probably never figure it out. She laid her hand against his warm chest, his hair an intriguing texture under her palm. "I'm probably going to drive you crazy running hot and cold, Denver. My life has been...very different from yours."

"Tell me."

"You don't want to hear it, trust me. You'd run screaming from the bed."

"The only direction I could run where you're concerned is toward you. And the only screaming I could possibly do is in the bed when I'm inside you."

"Mmm. That sounds nice." Her lips curved on their own into a sappy smile; she allowed herself a glance up at him, which didn't kill her or reduce her to instant victimhood, so she looked up again. His eyes were dark, warm and peaceful and she lingered, then reached and brushed a finger across the tips of his dark lashes, slid down the long noble springboard of his nose and landed on the smooth pad of his lips, tracing to each soft corner.

He whispered her name and moved closer, and she realized with a start that after all that had happened tonight this would be their first kiss. She squirmed with the irrational fear she was expert at but made herself stay motionless. He tasted her lips, bit gently, keeping the pressure soft and playful, doubtless understanding she didn't want intensity or passion. Denver knew her better than Ty ever did, even without knowing much about her at all. And he was probably seven trillion times more patient. Ty hadn't even known the meaning of the word. He'd gone from zero to furious in point eight seconds. His idea of foreplay had been "ready to get stuck?" and his idea of tenderness had been not being rough with her.

She left herself open to Denver's kisses, trying to keep at bay, not fear this time, but a longing to wrap her arms around him until they both got lost.

She knew she wouldn't. Her resistance was automatic, as if she'd given in to the fear and denied herself pleasure for so long she no longer knew how to go after it. For now she'd let him keep bringing the pleasure to her. It was enough. Maybe by some miracle it would be enough for him too for a while longer. At least until she could work on reversing a lifetime of conditioning.

He stopped kissing her and she felt her diaphragm restart, unaware she hadn't been breathing.

"Whatever you did, it's not going to scare me off, Lindsay."

"Whatever?" She raised her eyebrows comically high, wanting to keep the afterglow casual and manageable.

"Okay, if you encouraged children to play with gasoline and matches or gave heroin to puppies or—"

"Uh, no. I was an angel compared to that."

"I know." He was watching her carefully. She realized that the more she held back, the more of an issue her past would become.

"Let's just say I wasn't very discerning in my choice of partners."

"I wasn't very discerning in my choices either. If they were female and willing, that was enough for me." He frowned thoughtfully. "You know, even a convincing drag queen might have worked."

She laughed and he grinned and kissed her again, this time slightly longer, slightly more pressure, a real kiss, a round-trip kiss—one that zinged all the way down and again coming back up.

The kiss ended, and she felt loss along with the relief. "That's not so shocking. What else you got?"

"I did my share of abusing substances."

"Ah." He fell onto his back, clasped his hands under his head, which contracted his arm muscles nicely. "Wasted lives come in all shapes, sizes and income levels. At least you turned yours around. Till high school, when my parents moved, I grew up in a small, wealthy white suburb. The people not only had plenty of money but a sense of entitlement so profound they knew they'd never miss the brain cells they killed because someone would keep handing them the good life even if they could barely function on their own."

She rolled onto her side to look at him and let her fingers follow the hard rolling hills of his biceps and shoulders. She knew what he was doing. Trying to minimize the differences between them and as futile as it was, she loved him for it. *Liked* him for it. Liked him very, very much. "That sounds grim."

"I guess it was. But when it's all you've known, you accept it as the way things are and plow gamely on." He extended the arm near her head and scooped her close to lie against him. "What other horrors have you to disclose?"

I killed my last boyfriend and I'm being blackmailed for it. "I left home at seventeen."

"Eighteen."

"Huh?" She raised her head to look at him.

"I left home at eighteen."

"Oh." She rolled her eyes and poked his side. "Right. To go to some Ivy League college. Living the rough life there, weren't you? Never knew where your next A plus would come from? Roaming the streets at night in search of hot women in need of cooling, constantly in danger of being attacked by professors with questions you couldn't answer…"

"Yeah, okay, you win that one." He pulled her down again and kissed the top of her head. "I've had a lot of opportunities, most of which would have been open to you too, if you'd wanted them enough and had known how to go about getting them. But yeah, I don't deny a lot of things are easier with money and a certain type of upbringing. A lot of things."

She bristled at the idea that she could have had what he had by wanting it enough. He had no idea. But then she hadn't wanted anything at seventeen except to escape her parents. All her life she'd run from things. Not until she got the job at Chassy and started working her way up did she find a life to look forward to instead of to leave behind.

Being born into money meant more than cash. It encompassed attitude, and as he'd said, a sense of entitlement. People like Denver went to Yale because it was expected of him. People like Lindsay didn't because it had never even occurred to her to try.

"What else, Lindsay? Tell me about your parents."

"You first."

He lunged suddenly, toppling her. "You're not going to get out of it that easily. *You* first."

She grinned up at him. God, this was fun. She'd forgotten how much fun all the early excitement was between lovers, when everything was young and beautiful and possible. Before you found out the dark secrets and evil that existed in everyone. It was so hard to believe Denver had his share too.

"C'mon, tell."

She laughed. "It's not a pretty story. My mother was intent on making sure I knew every day what a disappointment I'd turned out to be."

He cringed. "Nice."

"It was a relief to find out I was adopted." Last

summer she'd had to read the letter from Daisy Winfield three times before it sank in that someone else could lay claim to the title of Lindsay's mother. Then it took four or five times through Daisy's description of her daughters before it registered that Lindsay had a real family—right here in Boston.

Lindsay released a long breath, feeling again a stab of regret that her birth mother had died of cancer before Lindsay had gotten to meet her. "A huge relief."

"I remember. Not that you actually *told* me." He rolled his eyes and grinned. "But you were clearly happier after you found out. And even more so after you found your sisters."

And even more so now. She wanted to say it. She really did. But it stuck in her throat and she had to glance away from him. Who knew what their relationship would entail after tonight? Lindsay knew that the first night was no indicator of how a couple would get along. She and Denver still had to work together. If they had any common sense, they'd leave tonight alone and go back to being friends. Though she had a feeling now that the chemistry between them had been unleashed there'd be no going back.

The thought alarmed her, though not as much as she expected.

"How did you cope growing up?"

"You'll be shocked."

He looked instantly wary. "What?"

"I retreated inside myself."

Denver cracked up and she found herself feeling lighter and freer than she had in forever. She wanted this moment to go on and on, for Gina to choke on a hot dog or get pushed accidentally onto the T tracks.

"I read a lot. My grade school librarian was like my drug supplier, constantly providing me with fixes so I could escape."

"What kind of books?"

"Adventure, romance, classics, anything as far away as possible from my life."

"Tell me about your favorite."

"Oh." She smiled. "That's easy. My favorite was *A Little Princess*. It's about a girl at an exclusive boarding school whose father dies suddenly. She's banished to the school's attic and forced to become a scullery maid. A wealthy neighbor sees her and has his servant creep into her room at night so she wakes up each morning to hot food and a fire. Each day new furniture and decorations mysteriously appear in the attic. It seemed so magical to me, that transformation of her bleak life."

She heard her voice thicken and cleared her throat. "I read it again when I was much older and realized it's sentimental slop. But I still love the story."

"I can see why. You've done that to your own life." He rubbed his chin contemplatively. "So what about dear old Dad?"

"He took his cue from Mom for the most part." She recalled her small round father, his thick glasses and greasy dark comb-over. A study in contrast with her tall, gaunt, chain-smoking mom. "He liked his drink in the evening. Sometimes it made him mellow, sometimes it made him…mean."

"Mean." His body tensed. Lindsay was struck again by how much he understood without her having to say it. "So you left. And were not discerning in your romantic choices."

"Right." She stared at the hair on his chest. Though unable to meet his gaze she could practically hear the thunk, thunk of all the pieces falling into place in his brain.

"They hit you. The men."

Tears started in her eyes. She swallowed, swallowed again. Her mouth opened and nothing came out. *Come on, Lindsay. It's safe. You can do this for God's sake, form the words and say them.* "Not all. Just the last one."

He rolled away and for one horrifying second, she thought he'd rejected her already, that he couldn't bear being with a woman stupid enough to submit to that kind of treatment. How could someone in his position understand how her view of herself was so low back then she half thought she deserved it?

How could Mr. Yale ever understand that depth of self-loathing?

"I'd like to kill him." His voice was flat but the power of the anger behind it thrilled her as much as the irony made her want to laugh. *Too late, I already did.*

"He's ancient history."

"Lindsay." His tone told her he was about to ask something important and she got nervous. "Is that why you freaked when I was rough with you on the couch last night?"

She did laugh that time, partly because the question

was so unexpected and so much easier than she'd been afraid it would be. "I thought I hid that."

"From ordinary people you might have." He rolled back toward her, started unbuttoning her pajama top. "But I, Denver Langston, have made it my expert secret mission over the past year to decipher the fascinating enigma that is Lindsay Beckham."

He pushed the flannel of her pajamas to the side, exposing her skin to the room's chill, making his stroking hand feel even warmer. She arched as his fingers slid over her breast. When he kissed her, moving over her, she tried to feel cocooned and protected, wrapping her arms around him, giving herself over to whatever could be between them.

Instead, she started to feel the panic being powerless always induced in her and wriggled to one side, trying to get free.

Immediately he lifted off her, put a hand to her waist to stop her sliding away and turned her so they were face-to-face. "Better?"

She nodded. How did he understand her so well? "Are you like this with all your other women?"

"All what other women?" He brushed his finger along her cheek. "There's only you, Lindsay."

She pushed away the double flip of thrill and fear at the thought of being the only woman he wanted. "I meant women before. Are you always this intuitive?"

"No." He looked puzzled. "I'm usually an asshole."

"Come on." She laughed and he grinned in response. "Be serious."

"I grew up a lot, after leaving my life of what you'd call immense privilege, and grew up more this past year, after leaving my career in L.A. I had one serious relationship early on. After that, women were…" He frowned and lifted a hand. "Uh, how do I put this? I didn't allow myself to care about them first, as friends. I pursued them as…"

"Intellectual beings?"

His turn to laugh. "Exactly. You and I were friends first. You snuck up on me. I have no idea when."

"Last night?"

"I wouldn't call that sneaking." He waggled his eyebrows. "I'd call that open attack."

"Okay, okay." She nudged playfully at his shoulder. "Not my subtlest hour."

"One of your sexiest."

"You think?" She batted her eyelashes, flirting shamelessly. But it didn't feel like flirting she'd ever done before. Not like the desperate uploading of her sex appeal for other men, hoping for a meal, a drink, a hit of something or a place to stay for a night, a week, a month. Underneath that flirting had lurked fear and self-hatred, though at the time she hadn't seen it.

What a huge part of her life she'd screwed up. Lindsay's Painful Past—the gift that kept on giving.

"Well…" He kissed her again, keeping space between their bodies, his hand lightly stroking her side. "It *was* your sexiest…until tonight."

She reached between them and found his penis, gliding her fingers along its hardening length.

"Lindsay?"

Her hand stilled. Again with the serious tone. She'd been pushed about as far into happy couple land as she could take right now. She wanted this evening to stay in the flirty mood they'd just discovered. She wanted more sex, then she wanted to be alone to sleep and think everything over.

"What?" She didn't even try to hide the dread in her tone.

"Something's been bothering you for the past few months. I'm not going to shut up until you at least give me a hint. So you might as well start with that now."

"An ultimatum?" She turned away. "I don't do ultimatums."

"Geez, Lindsay." He took her hand and squeezed it. "I care about you. And unless I'm a complete fool, which wouldn't be the first time, you care about me, at least some. If our positions were reversed, if you knew I was hurting badly over something, wouldn't you want to help me?"

"I'd figure it was your business, Denver, to tell me or not. I'd respect you for your choice if you made it abundantly clear that you didn't want to."

"Okay. That didn't work. Let me put it this way. I'm a guy. And in all guys, however enlightened, there dwells a caveman hero whose job it is to protect his woman."

"Oh, please. What century—"

"While women, on the other hand, would clearly offer us up for sacrifice at the first sabre-toothed opportunity."

"We're no dummies."

"Listen." He spooned up behind her, and the cave-woman part of her that she could never quite get rid of, thrilled to his warmth and size. He laid his hand gently on her shoulder. "If you're in trouble, I want to know."

"You're a pest, Denver." She knew her tone said otherwise.

"A pest who can't stand watching you suffer like this." He kissed her hair, then the warm hand on her arm became a warm hand at her elbow, traveling across her stomach and down between her legs. "Tell me."

"Sexual bribery?"

"Whatever works." His voice was deep and soft in her ear. His fingers were heating up her whole body. She should stop him, twist away and take a stand once and for all.

"What is it, Lindsay?" He slid a finger gently along her sex, used the moisture to slip around her clitoris. "Tell me."

Her breath was coming less evenly. She felt her legs spreading of their own accord. He grabbed her thigh and hooked her top leg back over his. "Just say the words. It's so easy."

Her face flushed; she gave a tiny moan. His finger slipped inside her, then two, mimicking the sex rhythm. From time to time he stopped and circled her clit again.

She felt her orgasm starting to build, impossibly soon after he started touching her. She made a low, inarticulate sound and clutched a fistful of her pillow.

"Tell me," he whispered urgently. "Tell me."

"Denver." Her voice was a plea. He thrust his fingers harder and she bucked up against them.

"Ple-e-ease." His tone was low.

"No." She thrashed and tossed her head...on the brink...on the brink... *"No."*

His fingers stopped, he whispered her name and in a second he'd turned her and slid inside, thrusting ferociously as if he wanted to catch up to her ecstasy.

She clutched him, dug in with her fingers and imprisoned his legs with hers, straining up toward the climax. She felt her body gathering force as if she were about to leap across some huge, impossible distance. Then it launched, a low burn that rose and rose, hit a plateau and broke apart into contractions nearly as intense as the wave that swept her there.

He made a deep animal sound and pulled out of her, stroked himself a few times and spilled warmth onto her belly.

Silence except for their ragged breaths.

"You okay?" he asked finally.

She laughed, a short burst that was more about irony than humor. "Does a body-exploding orgasm count as okay?"

"Uh, yeah. Sort of. It's not bad anyway." He reached for tissues from the box next to her bed, cleaned them both up and lay next to her.

This time the silence was full of slowing breathing and too many unspoken words. Then suddenly she was talking.

"It has to do with...an old friend, who is...giving me trouble. That's all."

His body stiffened, but she didn't know what he was

thinking lacking his uncanny ability to read her every expression and thought.

"Is there anything I can—"

"No. No. It's all under control. I'm fine." Already she regretted telling him. He'd want to find out who, what, why. And when he did, she'd lose the rest of herself and have nothing to stand on if he withdrew.

He sighed, and she heard his frustration and couldn't blame him. "If you say so."

More silence, more words she knew she owed him. These would be easier to say. "I'm sorry. I'm…trying."

"I know you are. And I'm trying to be patient." He squeezed her close to him. "But everyone knows doctors make terrible patients."

"And terrible jokes." Lindsay shifted closer. "You're incredibly patient. I probably couldn't be in your place."

"You're worth it," he whispered. "Now it's late. Let's get some sleep."

Sleep? She felt her eyes widen in alarm. As in spend the whole night together, wake up together, have breakfast together, plan the day together and the next day and the week after that as long as they both shall live?

Calm down, Lindsay.

"I want to hold you all night."

Oh no. No holding. Holding was bad. Lindsay liked to sleep alone, with no one bothering her or taking up space.

"I make a great omelet, too." He yawned and put his hand to her cheek.

No omelets. She wanted him gone, she wanted him

out of here. Now. This was getting way too intense, way too personal, way too much like boyfriend and girl-friend, when she'd come to him only with the need to fulfill the dare and get her jollies in the process.

Right. She was just a sexual barracuda who hadn't felt a thing in her heart all night. She'd confided in him because she didn't trust or care about him at all.

Damn it.

But spending the night... It was too soon. Yet how could she force him out into the freezing city to find himself a cab at this hour on a Friday night? And she couldn't exactly ask him to sleep on the couch.

"You want me to go?"

"No." She said the word automatically to be polite but in the next second that *no* registered as the truth. Part of her wanted him to stay, the tiny scared part that was so unused to getting its way it didn't even know how to ask for intimacy, for happiness, for healing love.

"No." She said it again, more certainly. "You can stay." At least for tonight. Then...

She sighed and didn't resist when he wrapped his arm over her, drawing the covers over them both.

Only one thing was certain. She had never been this confused about how she felt about someone. Not her parents, not the mother she'd never met who gave her away, not Ty, no one.

Denver Langston held that honor all by his sexy self.

7

DENVER WALKED DOWN NEWBURY STREET in the biting
cold among throngs of lunch hour shoppers. He was on
his way to meet Brooke at O.M. Worthington, a ven-
erable department store near Copley Square where she
worked. He'd invited her to lunch to talk about Lindsay.
After having been so sure Lindsay was finally thawing
on Friday night, he'd wanted to beat his head against a
wall when the next day and yesterday Lindsay acted as
if nothing had happened between them. Brooke obviously needed to talk about Lindsay too because she
hadn't sounded surprised when he told her why he
wanted to meet. In fact, she'd sounded relieved.

Something else had fueled his desire to pry further
into the sexy, alluring and often infuriating mystery
that was Lindsay. Last night he'd gone to dinner at his
friend Jack Harmon's house. He'd known Jack since
high school where they'd raised harmless hell together.
Jack was married now, teaching at Harvard, living in a
small but gorgeous house in Cambridge within walking
distance of the university and Harvard Square. His wife,
Heidi, had just found out she was pregnant with their

second child. They'd both been glowing. Their son Peter—two and three-quarters he'd solemnly informed Denver—had been charmingly rambunctious.

When Jack had echoed Denver's compliments on the meal and raised a toast to his wife, his eyes sending her enough warmth to melt the polar ice caps, Denver's veal had suddenly lost its flavor. Being with someone, making a home together, raising children entered his mind for the first time since he'd been engaged to Jenna.

He wanted a wife and a kid or two, dinners in their house—home—surrounded by the gooey glow of love and contentment. He tried to picture himself in such a life with Lindsay, and came up empty. Instead of serenity and intimacy, he saw frustration, dissatisfaction and arguments—great makeup sex aside.

Except…trying to imagine his life without her didn't work either.

He'd even thought of talking to Jack about Lindsay, had worked the conversation around to how Jack and Heidi met and fell in love. Hearing their story again only underlined what a mistake it would be to consult Jack. His and Heidi's attraction had been immediate, their dating blissful and relatively conflict-free, their engagement and wedding a sure thing.

Appealing to a man in Jack's position for advice on love was like asking advice on his golf game from a beginner who scored a hole-in-one his first day out. Jack had gotten it right the first time effortlessly. He wouldn't know squat about the agonies Denver was going through. He'd say, "If it's right, it feels right, and you'll know it."

Love couldn't always be that simple.

Denver was a scientist. Problems had treatment options, solutions. Some he arrived at by following hunches or his instincts. But at its heart, surgery wasn't all that different from auto mechanics. Tissue, bone and blood generally behaved as expected. The same parts were found on the same bodies in the same places. Carefully controlled research produced results that corroborated a hypothesis or didn't. Nothing in his dozen plus years of schooling and practice had prepared him for the complications involved in the problem that was Lindsay.

What had happened between the morning they ate breakfast together and that afternoon when he got to work? Lindsay had shown no indication that anything romantic had gone on between them. Who was this *friend* giving her trouble? What kind of trouble? Was it her last boyfriend? The abusive one? Was he threatening her? Denver's body tensed with the urge to defend her. With violence, if necessary. Again, not like him. He was a reasonable person, able to stay calm and rational in times of crisis.

Why wouldn't Lindsay let him help?

Another option raised its sickening head. Maybe this boyfriend's reentry into her life wasn't unwelcome. Maybe the *trouble* had to do with her conflicting feelings for whoever-he-was and for Denver. Maybe she did sleep with Denver only because of the dare and the next night she was back in the arms and bed of a man who knew her better. At work over this past weekend she'd been her usual friendly and busy self but avoided being alone with him. She wouldn't go swimming or to his place. She wouldn't share a drink or a meal. She forced smiles, chatted superficially and moved off as soon as it was polite. When his one attempt at talking about their night together was met with her patented stonewall, he'd backed off to give her space, his usual good guy routine. But frankly, his well of patience was about dry.

He muttered a word not appropriate to polite society, horrifying a woman passing with her toddler in a stroller.

"Sorry." He lifted both hands in apology, then jammed them back into the warm pockets of his jacket, forcing his breathing to return to normal.

As if all this wasn't complicated enough, at dinner the night before Jack had mentioned a mutual friend of theirs from high school, Alec Swanson, who'd been at medical school at Brown with Denver also specializing in plastic surgery. His long-time business partner was retiring from the clinic. Apparently Alec had been very interested to hear that Denver was in town and wanted to talk to him about his career plans. Denver would be a fool not to jump at the chance to join an established practice with a man whose work and ethics he so admired.

But that would mean leaving Chassy and turning his back on Lindsay when she needed him most. Unless it turned out to be when she needed him least.

This was nuts. He was making himself crazy invent-ing torturous possibilities for her behavior without a shred of evidence that any of his theories held the tiniest grain of truth.

He needed that evidence. His sanity was starting to depend on it. More than that, he needed to act. Being Mr. Nice Guy had gotten him nothing but ready to give up. He loathed that he'd have to betray her confidence to Brooke. Still, if he didn't get some answers, he was either going to make an even bigger fool out of himself over Lindsay than he already had or leave Chassy and find a job in his field and a woman who'd meet him halfway. Talking to Brooke was his last-ditch effort. If she knew nothing, and all she could recommend was more patience, he was done.

Nearing Copley Square now, he made himself concentrate on the upscale charm of Newbury Street shops and brownstone apartments. Reaching the imposing stone building that housed O.M. Worthington, he grinned. There was Brooke in one of the store's front windows. Her very nice rear was showcased as she bent down to adjust her titillating red-and-white lingerie display, Sweet Nothings. He had to say it was an enticing combination of sex and elegance—like Brooke herself. Pretty racy for the stodgy store. Brooke was doing good things for O.M. Worthington, which could use a kick into the twenty-first century.

Still grinning, he pushed in. The interior was warm, and smelled vaguely of the too-heavy perfume an overly made-up woman was using to attack female shoppers.

"Hey, Brooke." He peeked around to where she was redistributing fake snow dotted with crimson hearts on the floor of the display. "You're giving shoppers quite a view. I recognized you immediately."

She shot him the expected—and deserved—dirty look and stood, careful not to bump her head on the hanging strands of blinking snowflakes and glowing red hearts. "Thanks, Denver. The snowflakes went out and I had to do an emergency repair."

"Well, it looks great. Even without your...assets."

She laughed and stepped out of the window, accepting his arm for assistance, a tiny red heart loosening itself from her fuzzy cream sweater and fluttering to the floor. "I'll wash my hands, sign out and be ready in five, okay?"

"Okay." He busied himself examining merchandise including a particularly lethal-looking pair of high heels in the shoe department imagining Lindsay in them...and nothing else.

Since when was he a masochist?

Exactly five minutes later, Brooke strode back toward him, her height making her easily visible, though she was shorter than Lindsay, probably by all of an inch. Her resemblance to her half sister was striking. Same widow's peak—though Brooke's hair was brown, not blond—same high cheekbones and wide mouth. Same graceful stride. Of course in his eyes, she wasn't as beautiful as Lindsay, nor as sexy, but he'd bet her boyfriend David felt differently.

"You're right on time." He tapped his watch, impressed.

"I'm good that way. Shall we?" He followed her into

the frigid sunlight down the block toward Clarendon Street and into a casual sandwich place, which suited him fine.

"Thanks for meeting me." He spoke after they'd settled at a small table toward the back of the restaurant.

"You're welcome. I'm especially happy you called this morning because an old friend of my mother's, Reba Koldowski, has been pestering me for a lunch date."

"Not one of your favorite people?"

Brooke tipped her hand rapidly one way then the other, *comme çi, comme ça.* "She's very sweet. And she was very good to Mom. But she's…better in small doses. Loves to gossip, knows *every*thing about *every*one. Apparently she has something extra-juicy to tell me. Again."

"And you don't want to know?"

She rolled her eyes. "Last time it was that she suspected her brother-in-law's son is gay. It was all I could do not to say, 'Who cares? Let the man be who he is.'"

He chuckled, glad for this chance to get to know one of Lindsay's sisters better. "I can imagine."

"Anyway, I won't be able to put poor Reba off forever but you gave me a legitimate excuse today and I'm grateful."

"Glad to help." He took a sip of water, wondering how soon he could turn the subject around to Lindsay without being too obvious.

"So." She clapped her hands, then rubbed them together. "I take it you're worried about Lindsay."

He nodded, grateful she'd come right to the point. "You could say that."

"We're all worried about her."

Denver shifted uneasily. "I don't like going behind her back to talk about her, but—"

"Let me guess." Brooke held up a hand to stop him. "You can't get Lindsay to tell you anything."

"Bingo."

Brooke nodded, her brown eyes troubled. "She's a tough one. I've come to love her over the past months. There's a bond between us that...well, I don't know, these things defy explanation. It's not like we spill our darkest secrets daily. You know that's not her style. But it's there."

"Has she—" He cleared his throat. Not a big mystery why he was having trouble asking this question. "Has she recently mentioned a *friend* coming back into her life?"

"You mean a male friend?" Brooke looked astonished. "Like a boyfriend?"

"I assume."

"That seems really unlikely."

Her genuine surprise eased his fear but only somewhat. Given Lindsay's nature, it was entirely possible Brooke just didn't know. He sighed and pushed wearily at his menu. "I feel like a jerk passing along something she told me. To be honest, I'm pushed to the wall here. She's holding something back. Something big. And it's killing me she won't tell me what it is."

"I understand. Believe me, I do. I've only known her since September so I have nothing to compare her behavior to. It doesn't take much, though, to figure out something is troubling her. I'd like to help. All of us would. I know you would too, Denver."

"Yeah." His voice came out husky. "Though I'm starting to wonder if she'll ever let me."

A tired-looking waitress asked for their orders as if they were annoying her by eating at the restaurant. Since he hadn't been paying attention to the menu, Denver told Brooke to go ahead. She ordered the daily soup special of curried cauliflower and a salad. Distracted, he asked for the same and added a grilled cheese sandwich.

"You were telling me something you had finally gotten out of her…" Brooke prompted.

"Yeah." He grimaced, hating this feeling of betrayal even more than he knew he would. "She said a friend of hers was giving her trouble."

"Hmm." Brooke frowned. "What kind of trouble?"

"I have no idea." He couldn't tell Brooke his worst fear. She was already plenty worried about her sister. "I was hoping she'd said something to you."

"No. You think an old boyfriend is harassing her?"

"Possibly."

"Why wouldn't she say something? Why would that have to be a secret?"

"It wouldn't. The other possibility is that he has shown up out of the blue just as she and I were…" He cleared his throat again. "Getting closer."

Brooke tilted her head, looking puzzled. "And so you think…what?"

"That maybe she's conflicted." He wanted to groan at how miserable he sounded. To hell with his sleeve, his heart was sitting in the middle of his forehead with a big target painted on it.

"No. Absolutely not. They way she looks at you—it's as if other men don't exist. Joey and Katie look at Sebastian and Liam that way. I don't need a mirror to know I look at David that way too. If she's not in love with you yet, it's only a matter of time."

He squelched the thrill of hope with a scowl. "Or a matter of her determination to beat it."

Brooke winced. "Self-sabotage. Yeah, I worry about that."

"Gee, not me."

Brooke laughed, and even her laughter reminded him of Lindsay, though Brooke's was a lot easier to come by.

"Okay." She folded her hands and thumped them onto her place mat. "I'm going to be blunt here. The three of us have tiptoed around Lindsay for months. We were all concerned about her. We all did the most we could to let her know that we love her, that we consider her family and that we're here for her if she ever needs us. I'm sure you've done the same."

"Yup." Except for the part about family and about love. Too soon for that. For her, anyway. God he had to be the world's biggest fool to fall for this woman above all others.

"Katie, Joey and I got together early this month and decided this stalemate could go on forever. And that in our opinion what Lindsay really needed was a push. No, a shove."

"In which direction?"

"Yours."

"Ah." He actually grinned. "Yeah, she told me I had you to thank."

"You're welcome." Brooke's smile was as warm as her eyes. "By the way, I haven't had a chance to say that I'm really happy for you. For both of you."

Denver's grin faded. Happy. Yeah, he'd been happy too for about twelve hours. Then Lindsay had made it clear that love was love. but her dare was a dare and never the twain would meet. "I wouldn't plan the ceremony yet."

"No, no. I know. Sorry. I know how she is." She fanned herself. "I got carried away."

Not any more than he had been. "So you think we've been going too easy on her."

"I do. We all do. She obviously didn't have the kind of upbringing we did." Her voice dropped into regret. "You know, I'm actually glad in a small way that Mom died before she found out what Lindsay's adoptive parents were like. The guilt of having given her child away into a life of hardship…she never would have gotten over it."

Denver nodded, his heart aching at the thought of Lindsay raised by the Winfields even though John Winfield wasn't her father, the way Brooke had been. John and Daisy could have given Lindsay all those opportunities she missed and so deserved.

Would she have grown up more like Brooke? Open? Easily emotional? Prone to laughter?

Waste of time pondering what might have been.

"Anyway, my point was that she didn't grow up with anyone she could trust." Brooke's face showed the pain she was feeling. "She needs to understand that the world won't end if she shares her troubles with people who love her."

"More to the point, their love won't end."

"Exactly. I'm convinced deep down she knows she can trust us. It's like we're the firemen standing on the ground with the net and she's in the burning building. She can see us. She knows we're there for her. It's just getting to the point where she can make herself jump."

The waitress brought their food, and conversation stopped while she distributed the plates and in a flat, bored monotone hoped they'd enjoy their lunch.

The second she stepped away, Brooke leaned in, spooning up her soup. "All I'm saying is that if someone is giving her trouble and we decide to wait until she tells us… Well, who knows. It could be annoying trouble but it could also be dangerous. Lindsay would act the same either way."

"Right." He dipped into his soup with zero appetite; undoubtedly delicious, to him it tasted like faintly spiced library paste. "I've given her every opportunity to tell me. Trust me, I'm bordering on being obnoxious."

She gave him a sad smile. "She's lucky she has you. I think she's starting to realize it."

"But still won't admit it." He sighed. "I'm lousy at sitting back and waiting. In fact, Sitting Back And Waiting was the only course I failed in college."

Brooke clapped her hand over her mouth to keep from spitting soup. "Warn me next time you're going to do that."

"Sorry." He grinned at her. He liked Brooke a lot. She

was smart, spirited and seemed to have good instincts, which only confirmed his fear that Lindsay could be in danger. He scooped up another spoonful of the soup and found the second tasted much better. "I liked your fireman image. Someone needs to get behind Lindsay on that burning building's ledge and give her a push."

"Absolutely." Brooke nodded firmly. "The three of us think likewise. We've tried clean and polite. Now we have to get dirty. Invade her privacy. Snoop shamelessly. Talk to people she knows. Tail her if necessary. Break into her office and examine all her papers."

"Uh, Brooke?"

"Okay, I watch too much TV. But you get my drift. The thing is I get the feeling some of her past was a little…" She waved her spoon in a circle as if beckoning her next words. "Self-destructive."

"And you're worried she's on a path to self-destruct again. I am too."

"God forbid we ever had regrets about not stepping in. Not when she's someone we care about so much."

"Amen." Finally, something he could do. He attacked his soup with relish.

"So." Brooke looked at him expectantly. "Do you want to push her off the building or should we?"

"I'll do it. Whatever it takes." He put out his hand to her. "You're family. You're forever. You have too much to lose if it backfires."

"Oh, come on, Denver." Brooke's eyebrow shot up and he knew what was going to come out of her mouth before it did. "Like you're the slightest bit different?"

8

"YOU'RE BEING KIDNAPPED."

Lindsay raised her eyebrows. All three of her half sisters had shown up at the bar just after she had arrived. It was nearly three, later than usual, but she'd been in a strange mood today, restless and without her usual discipline. February was teasing Boston with one of those rare thaws that made everyone itchy for spring to get started.

She'd spent most of the day reading a book Katie loaned her, a sexy, wry look at postdivorce dating, and it had made her feel irreverent and very un-boss-like. More like the old party girl Lindsay. God forbid.

But business was business and right now she needed to change the schedule to reflect the new waitress hire and to order more pomegranate juice among other supplies. The Valentinis had been such a hit at the Martinis and Bikinis meeting she'd put them on the permanent drink menu.

"Kidnapped? I don't think so."

"Oh, but we do." Joey leaned against the door to her office, smirking. "We're taking you shopping."

"I have everything I—"

"We beg to differ." This from Katie, beaming up at Lindsay from her five foot three height, making Lindsay feel like an Amazon.

Lindsay couldn't help smiling back. "I have things I have to—"

"Leave them." Brooke shrugged as if her remark was so obvious she shouldn't even have had to make it.

"Do them later."

"Get someone else."

Lindsay sighed exaggeratedly. These Winfields were formidable. Used to getting their way. Used to rushing off on a whim and assuming other people would pick up any mess they'd left behind. They were as different from Lindsay as eggs Benedict from oatmeal, pâté from scrapple, tenderloin from Spam. And they were probably exactly what she needed. Especially today.

"I don't suppose I'll be able to object to this little scheme any more than I've been able to object to any of the others."

"Nope." Brooke swept Lindsay's worn red coat off the back of the door where it had been hanging and held it out. "You're ours for the next two hours."

"Two hours?" She looked at her watch. "I'll give you forty-five minutes tops. I have to be here when we open so I can—"

"That's why you hired such good staff." Joey grabbed the coat from Brooke and helped Lindsay into it. She considered resisting but couldn't quite make herself.

"I'll have to call Denver and ask him to—"

"Done." Katie waved her cell phone. "He's on his way."

"Honestly." She couldn't help laughing. "Don't you three ever—"

"Nope," Joey said helpfully.

"—let me finish my sentences?"

The Winfield sisters laughed. Brooke took Lindsay's right arm, Joey took her left, and escorted her firmly out of the bar onto the street into air that smelled like March and into—

"You have got to be kidding me."

A black stretch limo was parked outside the bar. A uniformed middle-aged man was holding the door politely open.

Katie giggled. "We knew you'd hate it. It was my idea."

"Well, thanks a whole lot." Lindsay shook her head and allowed herself to be escorted into the luxurious interior, tickled over the afternoon's developments in spite of herself. When was the last time she'd done anything with girlfriends except get drunk and troll for men? And this was the first time she'd taken time off to do anything with her half sisters. Hell, the first time she'd taken off, period.

Chassy would survive her short absence. And she'd owe Denver for taking over. In fact—her face grew red even at the thought—she could think of really fun ways to pay him back. For a few days after their night together, he'd been friendly, but aloof, maybe in reaction to her stupid panic over starting anything serious with him. She'd felt such a strong combination of attraction and fear that she'd barely been able to speak to him.

Then yesterday, early after lunch, she'd been wiping down a portion of the bar missed by the cleaning crew the night before, and he'd walked in, come straight over to her, backed her up against the wall and kissed her until she was barely able to stand. Even more astonishing, after releasing her, he'd winked and said, "Hi, Lindsay," and had gone into her office to hang his coat. After that? Business as usual. Except she hadn't come down to earth for the entire evening; every time their eyes met, she shot back up, like the man in the Mary Poppins movie her mom had taken her to on a rare pleasant outing, who was so full of laughter he floated up and hovered near the ceiling.

Finally, just after closing, tired and fretting over Gina, she'd come down, only to be grabbed and kissed again before he said good-night, leaving her staggering back this time. Unexpected and wonderful. Behavior she could get seriously used to.

Looking giddy with anticipation, her half sisters arranged themselves on the leather seats.

"How did you all get off work?" Lindsay leaned back, eyeing the assortment of compartments and buttons on the car sides, intending to enjoy pretending she rode in limos all the time.

"I'm at an important meeting." Joey buckled her seat belt, grinning. "Very, very important."

"I was taken terribly ill at lunch." Katie clutched her stomach anxiously. "I might not survive."

"Half a vacation day for me." Brooke sighed in amused exasperation. "Always by the book."

"Ha! The *Kama Sutra* maybe. We'll ask David," Joey teased.

Brooke sent her a scathing glance, then turned to Lindsay. "We started this adventure three years ago when none of us had boyfriends and Valentine's Day seemed like an evil plot to make us feel pathetic and single."

"Then it turned into an annual tradition." Katie shrugged off her coat and casually plucked a bottle of Veuve Clicquot out of a cooler next to her seat as if she— ho hum—spent most of her afternoons being driven in limos drinking expensive champagne. "We take an afternoon to go shopping and then have dinner together."

"Dinner?" Lindsay's stomach tensed. "You said two hours. I can't—"

"We know, we know you can't have dinner." Joey rolled her eyes. "There's got to be help for what ails you. Workaholics anonymous, something like that. Isn't there?"

Lindsay rolled her eyes right back at Joey, not even bothering to try to explain. This business was the first thing she'd ever been good at and she was going to make it work, whatever that took. The Winfields couldn't understand what it meant to work for a living, to depend on your success for survival, to have your identity wrapped up more in what you did than who you were. Not that her half sisters coasted through life on the family money, not by any means. Brooke had a thriving design career, Katie was a talented graphic artist and Joey, a successful lawyer. Still, with a fortune eternally growing in their bank accounts, they risked little more than pride if any ventures failed.

"So where are you taking me?"

"Back Bay," answered Brooke.

"Copley Place." Katie expertly eased the champagne cork out with a soft *thwunk* instead of the rowdy *pop* that spilled half the contents. "The mall, not the hotel."

Joey leaned toward Lindsay and waggled her eyebrows. "Victoria's Secret."

"We're all going to Victoria's Secret?"

"All going. All afternoon."

"To buy Valentine's Day presents for our menfolk." Brooke accepted her champagne as matter-of-factly as Katie was handing it out.

"And we are quite certain that Denver would love something too." Katie winked and poured for Joey.

Lindsay couldn't quite picture it. "What? A jockstrap with hearts on it?"

"Oh no." Joey shook her head and grinned wickedly, lifting her glass. "*We* get the lingerie. *They* get the present."

Lindsay's stomach sank. She made herself smile and take her cold glass of bubbly. Too much of her money and youth had been spent on and in sexy lingerie. Too young she'd learned that men responded so reliably to kinky underwear she didn't even have to bother with beauty or sparkling conversation or hell, even a personality. Like shooting fish in a barrel.

Unlike most women, her memories of lace and satin were painful and humiliating. That was a part of her life she no longer wanted anything to do with.

"A toast. To sisterhood and family and kinky thongs

that drive men wild." Katie hoisted her glass and the Winfields drank with enthusiasm.

Lindsay took a small sip and made herself nod appreciatively. She was sure it was the world's finest champagne but her taste buds weren't in the mood to celebrate.

"What's up, Lindsay? Not a good plan?" Brooke, as usual, saw through her determined pleasantness.

"No, it's great. It's a great tradition." She tried hard to sound enthusiastic but her voice was forced. Hollywood would never come knocking with an Oscar.

The energy and giddiness started draining out of the atmosphere.

"You're not still worried about leaving Chassy for a measly couple of hours, are you?" Joey gave Lindsay a disapproving look. "Because we could force you to stay out for *four* hours if we wanted to."

"Joey, honestly. We wouldn't do that to her. *Four* hours? No way." Katie bared her teeth in a killer smile. "But all night long? Yeah, *that* might work."

Joey and Katie laughed, and clinked glasses while Brooke rolled her eyes. "Now, children. As your eldest sister, I forbid you to—"

"Uh-uh, Brooke." Joey shook her head and pointed to Lindsay. "Think again."

"Second oldest." Katie giggled, but nervously. "Which means we don't have to listen to you anymore."

"Right. Sorry." Brooke flashed a cautious glance at Lindsay. "I guess I haven't gotten used to being second yet."

"Don't worry about it." Lindsay smiled warmly, but

for the second time in five minutes, she'd been the cause of awkwardness on this special occasion. Once again she felt like a wallflower among debutantes. However hard the Winfield sisters tried, it always came back to this: Lindsay wasn't one of them and never would be.

How could they understand the life she'd led? How could she explain why she wouldn't enjoy shopping for underwear? Though, if her lack of enthusiasm was affecting their mood on what was supposed to be a carefree outing, then she owed them an explanation. More than that, she couldn't—wouldn't—be the cause of their annual fun fizzling.

The limo purred up in front of the mall entrance on Huntington Avenue. The driver waited for another car to unload before he could pull close enough to the curb to let them out.

"Ready?" Brooke smiled bravely at Lindsay and flicked a glance at her sisters.

"No. Wait." Lindsay put her hands to her cheeks, then folded them in her lap. She could keep pushing her half sisters away by hiding who she was or she could tell the truth, risking rejection—but maybe bringing them closer. She knew what Denver would want her to do. And suddenly it was what she wanted too.

"The thing is…about the underwear." She spoke into the expectant silence. "I wore a lot of that stuff. For a lot of men."

Joey's eyebrows shot up. "Let me guess. On Martini Dares before you met us?"

"No. Years ago. On my own."

"Uh, professionally?" The color had drained from Katie's fair skin. Joey nudged her sharply and the color flew back in double. "I mean, sorry, I thought—"

"No, not professionally. I probably should have. Might as well have made it profitable." Her laugh was supposed to make light of her words but it came out bitter making the ensuing silence more painful.

This was why Lindsay didn't share. Her half sisters were her first ever family—the first one she'd ever wanted around—and she was terrified of not measuring up. If she had a nickel for every time her mother had made it clear that family didn't automatically mean love. That families could be broken. That she and her husband had taken Lindsay in, called her *Daughter,* indicating a supposedly sacred bond and obviously had lived to regret it.

"So I guess fun underwear isn't that special for you then, huh." Joey spoke without censure or disappointment, which made Lindsay feel worse.

She shrugged, biting her lip. *Good job, Lindsay.* Now she'd taken all the joy out of their afternoon. "You know, I'm sure it will be fine. I mean, wearing lingerie for Denver would be completely different. I know it would be."

She nodded earnestly and smiled, again aware she wasn't remotely convincing.

"I'm sorry that part of your past wasn't so great." Brooke laid a comforting hand on Lindsay's knee. "But yes, the best thing you can do is take the old associations away, so you don't have to deal with the horrible trauma of living the rest of your life without exciting underwear."

"God no." Joey kissed her fingertips and looked heavenward.

Katie nodded somberly, smile barely suppressed. "Amen."

Just like that? It was that easy? They made a few jokes and all was accepted and forgiven?

Except then she caught the Winfield sisters giving each other meaningful glances, a mouthed word here; a surreptitious nodding there; a brief murmur, Katie to Joey. What now?

"Lindsay. We learned something about our—about Mom a couple of weeks ago." Joey looked to her sisters, then back to Lindsay. "That is I found out and shared it with Brooke and Katie. We didn't tell you, because…well, the moment never felt right."

"And we weren't sure how it would make you feel since Mom gave you up for adoption…" Katie looked helplessly over at Brooke and fell silent.

Lindsay had to loosen her hold on her champagne glass. She didn't even know her mother, and she was already strangely agitated and strangely moved. "Just tell me."

"Our mom…" Joey drew a circle with her hands clearly meant to include all four of them. "When she met Dad, she was a professional escort. In fact it was how she met him. He needed a date to a party in Rhode Island."

"She was already pregnant with me, her second pregnancy…" Brooke glanced meaningfully at Lindsay. "She'd already had to give you away so she could keep working. She couldn't afford to stop."

"And apparently *her* mom, our grandmother…" Joey raised her eyebrows, expression and intonation comically bright as if the news was going to be super cheery. "…was a prostitute!"

Lindsay's mouth fell open; she let out a burst of laughter. Winfields? With such a background? Then the import of what they were saying hit and ludicrously, she laughed again. "So you think being a slut is in my blood?"

"Hey, it's in all of ours, Lindsay." Katie was grinning now. "We might have grown up in privilege compared to you, but our roots are all the same."

"And given how we all jumped on our Martini Dares, I'd say that wild streak has been simmering under the surface our whole lives, waiting for its chance." Joey raised her glass. "And I say here's to it."

"Absolutely."

"To hidden wildness." The women clinked and drank.

"Oh, speaking of which!" Katie held up her hand in excitement. "Tanya called me. Guess what?"

"Her lab partner?" Joey asked.

Katie nodded, beaming. "She didn't need a dare. She just walked right up to that boy and said, 'How 'bout you and me get outta here and suck down some milkshakes together?'"

Brooke covered her mouth to keep from spitting champagne. "Milkshakes! Oh, God, that's priceless!"

"Bet he didn't know what hit him."

"Apparently…" Katie grinned smugly. "He, ahem, *rose to the occasion* quite nicely."

"No! No way." Brooke squealed.

"That is fabulous. I'm really happy for her." Lindsay couldn't stop smiling.

"See? Told ya." Joey winked. "There's hidden wildness in all of us. Mom wasn't the beginning and you're not the end."

"We also found out that as much as she loved Dad, being a Winfield was hell for Mom sometimes. Especially with the family watching her every move." Brooke balanced her glass as the car moved forward again. "When she wanted to bust out, she and her friend Reba used to put on disguises so Mom wouldn't be recognized and cause a scandal, and they'd go out on the town and live it up. Dad let her because he adored her and wanted her to be happy. Still he did always send undercover bodyguards after them to make sure they didn't get into trouble."

"Reba said the guards were so obvious she and Daisy used to send them a steady stream of drinks at every bar or club they went to just to piss them off since they couldn't drink on the job." Katie savored a mouthful of bubbly. "Poor things."

"So the *point* is, in all seriousness, Lindsay, you have nothing to be ashamed of because we sure as hell aren't ashamed of anything we've done. Nor could we ever be ashamed of Mom." Joey's voice thickened. "And we hope this confession will help you get that RSVP to the Winfield Valentine's Day ball back in our possession with a big fat, 'I'd love to come' on it."

"Because you belong there," Katie added.

Her simple statement made Lindsay's eyes teary.

She blinked hard and stared down into her lap. "Thank you. I really appreciate you trying so hard to make me feel a part of the family."

"You *are* part of the family, dear." Joey cleared her throat of its huskiness and pointed out the window where the driver had maneuvered them up to the mall entrance. "So whadya say. You up for us granddaughters-of-a-hooker buying raunchy undies together?"

"With the understanding that we'll model them indecently for men we love in hopes of getting massively laid?"

"Girls…" Brooke snorted. "Lindsay, we're happy to go somewhere else if buying underwear isn't your thing."

"Absolutely," Joey added earnestly. "There are other places where we can find things to turn on the guys."

"Like Home Depot," Katie said.

The women dissolved into laughter and just like that the moment was over and good spirit restored. Lindsay had no idea how her half sisters managed to get through life as if everything was harmless enough to be joked away. She envied them not only their wit but also their absolute command of the forces around them, forces that had been buffeting Lindsay for so long she took her helplessness for granted. Maybe she could learn a thing or two from these Winfields. Or from Tanya, who though stricken with shyness hadn't needed a Martini Dare to go after what she wanted.

Lindsay thought of Denver seeing her in the lingerie. She imagined his eyes darkened, his gaze heated, his longing to touch her tripled. She knew she'd been putting him through hell by her inability to let him in close. She wasn't trying to put him through hoops, though doubtless he felt that way at times. She just stunk at getting close to people. And yet, she'd just shared something of herself with her half sisters and instead of being rejected, she'd been drawn closer into the fold, found unexpected common ground with these wonderful, slightly intimidating women who with their easy and immediate acceptance had slain one of her most feared demons.

Maybe she could slay more of them. As silly as it sounded, maybe exciting underwear was a step in the right direction.

Decision made she nodded firmly, took another sip of her champagne, which had magically started to taste delicious, and spread her arms to embrace her half sisters. "You're right. I'm ready. Bring on Victoria's Secret."

9

LINDSAY SMILED AS SHE turned the corner onto Beaumont Street and Chassy came into view. *Hello, beautiful!* Soon to be even more beautiful. Lindsay had just come back from a meeting with Ralph Gebring's Aunt Marie. She couldn't deny she was encouraged. Aunt Marie had poured tea, offered homemade cookies and told Lindsay way too many details about how her South Boston neighborhood had changed in the last six decades. But underneath the cute-old-lady trappings, Lindsay had sensed tough intelligence. When the talk had turned to Chassy, Aunt Marie had asked a lot of shrewd questions and examined Lindsay's business plan carefully.

In the end she'd said she was looking at a few other prospects and that she needed to check details with her lawyer. Just as Lindsay had started deflating over what sounded like a brush-off, Aunt Marie had given Lindsay an unexpected hug. Then she'd told her how much she'd always wanted a daughter and that she was excited about her business. All hopeful signs.

If only there were some way to get rid of the financial drain that was Gina. But Lindsay had spent a lifetime coping with adversity, was coping now and would continue to cope. She had no other choice.

She pushed into the bar, later than she usually got there for the second day in a row, but this time for a better reason than being restless and lost in a book. She paused in the entranceway, imagining that the renovations had been done—the larger meeting room for Martinis and Bikinis parties and whatever other private affairs she booked; the separate dance room and small stage for live bands with a swinging door to keep the noise somewhat contained so the bar area would be more suitable for socializing; the new chef scurrying around the remodeled kitchen to prepare more sophisticated dishes. South Boston was changing, and Chassy would keep pace.

She drifted forward, still smiling, still imagining. Two more steps into the bar and she saw him— Denver—busy behind the bar. He paused in the middle of whatever he was doing and smiled. She paused in the middle of taking her next step into the bar, smiled harder and there you had it. The kind of moment she'd someday look back at and say, "Darling, that was the first moment I loved you, only I didn't realize it at the time." Not that Lindsay was the type ever to say such a thing. But at the moment she was very glad that underneath the sensible navy business suit she'd worn for the meeting, she'd decided to put on the underwear she'd bought with her half sisters the day before, a black lacy bra and matching panties, both sprinkled with crimson roses. Pretty, feminine, suggesting sex, not promising it. Brooke had found the set and brought it over to Lindsay who'd been wandering bemusedly through the racks.

The minute she tried them on, she knew she'd found perfection. Because the style was more tasteful than the lingerie she used to wear, pricier and better quality. Because she was older and no longer the hurting girl-woman desperate for male approval. And because it was for Denver and no one else—not even if she lived to be a hundred and had dozens more lovers. This would always be for him.

Something had clicked in that dressing room, something that started with her initial confession to Denver and had continued in the limo with her acceptance by her half sisters. A tiny pebble rolling down a rocky hill had dislodged more pebbles, larger rocks, and one day she hoped, a whole landslide of crumbling rock until she could open herself up to true intimacy.

One pebble at a time.

Bolstered by the smile shared with Denver and her determination to change, Lindsay sailed through the evening, floated through, soared through, helping out the new waitress, laughing with the customers, feeling as if a wire connected her and Denver all night, zapping back and forth attraction and excitement. Each time their glances met, no more than two or three minutes seemed to go by before their glances met again.

She might as well admit she was crazy about him. Besotted, to quote one of her favorite book words—a word recognizable in print but which you never heard anyone say. The feeling was truly blissful. All the better for being experienced this time without the choking haze of drugs and alcohol and fear.

Which meant something had to be about to happen to screw everything up.

No. No. She needed to hold on to her new attitude, to remember how her half sisters had reacted—or barely reacted—to her confession, and how good it had felt to get even that small bit of her weighty past off her chest. The trip to Victoria's Secret had been a new high in her relationship with her half sisters. They'd even teased her gently about her past, a true indication of their comfort with her and what she'd told them, which she'd been so certain would be a shocking and potentially damaging bombshell.

Apparently she took herself and her importance way too seriously. Maybe it was time she lightened up a little.

And while she was giving herself a pep talk, why shouldn't she start expecting good things to happen to her? Why not now? So many other bad chapters of her life had ended—unemployment, lack of family, why not end the bad chapter on relationships too?

At closing time, the crackling messages between her and Denver started to positively sizzle. The last customer left. Then the last staff member. The last chair was up-ended on the last table, the last glass hung, the front door locked, lights turned off…

"So." He stood near the door of her office, dimly lit by

the streetlight coming in through the bar windows, hands on his hips, looking strong and slightly mysterious.

"So?" She faced him, three feet away, feeling warm and slightly breathless. Their voices, which an hour ago couldn't have been heard at full volume, sounded loud and echoey in the deserted space.

"Now that your dare is fulfilled I guess you don't need me anymore." His brief grin betrayed his confidence that there was much more to come between them. Starting in a matter of minutes.

"Nope." She took a swaggering step forward, feeling positively giddy since she had the same confidence now. "Used you up, now it's time to toss you out."

"That's that, huh?"

"Yep." Another step forward. "This cowgirl is moving on."

"Damn." He shook his head mournfully. "Been a good ride, though."

"You'll always be my favorite mount."

"Aw, shucks. You're just saying that to be shallow and sexist."

"Nah." She swaggered to a stop an inch away and looked into his eyes, for once not afraid to. "I really mean it. The wildest ride of my life."

"Yeah?" He moved forward; their bodies met, his chest warm against hers. "There's one problem with you moving on."

"What's that?" She was whispering now, hot and impatient already.

"I want you to be moving on...top of me."

"Oh?"

"I want that now in fact."

"Hmm." She frowned, pretending to consider, shuffled her feet the last inch to bring her pelvis flush against his. "Ooh, so you do."

"And often after that."

"Hmm. Quite…a problem." She barely got the words out.

"Any solution?"

"One. It might work."

"What's that?" He was whispering too, dark and male and thrilling.

"We'll go in my office…"

"And?"

"Mess it up."

"Whoa, *mess it up?* Are you sure?"

She winced, pretending to reconsider. "Maybe just move a few papers out of parallel alignment and call that messed up?"

"You're on." His arms came around her tightly, he half lifted her through the door of her office while she giggled at his eagerness. God, this was fun. Why had she resisted? Did she think surrendering to this man would turn her back into the woman she used to be? That woman was gone. This man was here.

He set her carefully on the edge of her desk and where she expected him to rip off her clothes and have at it, instead he pulled her against him and kissed her. And kissed her.

And kissed her.

His lips were warm and firm and inviting; he tasted like coffee and smelled faintly of aftershave and of Denver.

She clutched his shirt, returned his kisses, then wrapped her arms around him. Emotion swelled in her chest—tears? Joy? The feeling was so sweetly painful that she couldn't tell.

And the old familiar panic started.

No. Not this time. She wasn't going to sabotage this. She wasn't going to have to go back to losers and abusers, men she couldn't trust. Or worse, embrace permanent celibacy.

She closed her eyes, took herself to that cool, calm place where nothing troubled her, the moon's still surface. And when his warm hands slid up her shirt, brushed over her breasts in their new bra, her fear subsided…almost. She couldn't expect to rid herself of reflexes overnight. Denver was patient; he wouldn't press, wouldn't push, he'd be there for her while she fought and conquered her old demons one by one.

For now, she'd keep herself only as safe as she absolutely had to be.

So when he pushed her navy skirt up, hands spanning her legs, following the line of her inner thighs until his thumbs met and pressed gently against her sex, she drew in her breath and clung to his shoulders. When he knelt and circled her hips with his arms, gathered her to him and breathed moist heat through her flowery panties, Lindsay dropped her head, and let her body feel all it wanted to—but also allowed her heart just a taste. It would catch up. Soon she hoped.

He bunched the soft material and moved it to one side, leaving his tongue, warm lips and fingers to do their magic. She braced herself on the desk, sent a mug of pencils crashing to the floor and didn't care. He had her close to coming in less than a minute.

"Denver."

Her plea—or was it a warning?—must have registered. He stood, and before she could recover enough to touch him, had opened his pants, put on a condom with easy quick movements, returned to the edge of the desk and tipped her face up to his.

"Ready?" he whispered.

"Oh yes."

He watched her as he pushed slowly in; she held his eyes as long as she could before she had to drop them, to concentrate instead on his slow, sexy slide inside her. In this position, with her bottom solidly on the desk, she couldn't move, couldn't answer his thrusts. He had control of the pace, the motion, brought her within an inch of coming and kept her there, pushing, grinding, until she was panting and desperate to go over the edge.

Still he kept her there, changing his rhythm, now faster, now slow, pulling out nearly all the way, thrusting back in to the hilt. Her cries became cries of frustration. She wanted to come *now*. Because the longer he did this, the longer he made love to her, the harder it became to stay under control pretending this was about penis and pussy, and the more obvious it became that this was about Denver and about Lindsay.

He kissed her again, his rhythm slowed now. He

drew back and met her eyes and she knew something
had to give. She was going to start crying. She was
going to tell him she loved him. She was going to tell
him everything, and that would be…

What?

Giving too much of herself away too soon.

She leaned back on the desk to one side, to free her
other hand, and found her clitoris, rubbing hard in self-
defense.

"Lindsay…"

"I need to come." She sounded just short of hysterical.

He gave in, pushed harder. This was no longer a
tender moment. This was an out-and-out race for the
finish line.

Three seconds before she would have reached it, the
phone rang.

Gina. Crap. Oh no. Oh no. She'd want an answer on
her damn "raise."

Lindsay's eyes shot to Denver's and she saw his challenge. Of course he'd sensed her distress. He wanted to
know.

"Leave it." Her voice shook. She hoped vainly that
he'd put it down to excesses of passion. "If it's important she'll call back."

Ring.

"She?" Of course he jumped on her slip immediately, looking inexplicably relieved. What had he
thought?

"Or he, whoever."

"You know who it is."

"A wild guess."

Ring.

His eyes narrowed. Not buying it.

Ring.

Before she even registered what was happening, Denver pulled out of her and picked up the phone.

"No." She launched herself to stop him. Rather than answering the call, he put the receiver to her ear.

And watched.

He was going to stand there and listen.

Damn it, hadn't she just been crowing to herself that he'd never push, he'd never pry, that he took such pains to take the relationship at her pace?

"No." She shook her head furiously.

"Lindsay?" Gina's voice, sounding too interested. "What's going on? *No* what?"

"No, I can't talk now." She let her eyes plead with Denver. His expression didn't change.

"Oh, I bet you can. We have so much to talk about, after all. Have you had your meeting with the old lady yet?"

Lindsay gasped. How the hell had she known about that? "Are you—"

She almost said *having me watched?,* but how the hell could she say that now? She had to get rid of Denver. "Hang on a sec."

The phone away from her ear, she covered the mouthpiece. "Please. This is private."

He opened his mouth as if he were about to start the familiar arguments, then he stopped, nodded curtly, pulled his pants back up and walked out. A few seconds later, the front door of the bar opened, then closed.

Lindsay closed her eyes and bowed her head, stupidly thinking, of all things, that she never even got to show him her new underwear. What had she just been crowing about earlier in the evening about how there was no reason for her luck to turn bad this time?

Maybe she was cursed. The daughter her mother had given away.

She put the phone back to her ear, near tears. "I'm here."

"Is there someone else there? Denver? Has he gotten into your pants yet? Did I interrupt him trying?"

Lindsay started to feel extremely sick. How did Gina know all this? Who was she talking to? Was someone betraying Lindsay? "No."

"No to which question?"

"All of them. How do you know Denver?"

"Honey, I know everything about you. He is supremely hot. We've had a few encounters of our own, you know. If he ever asks you to go swimming, trust me, do it. He's *so* worth it."

Ice. Her melting heart immediately turned to ice. She slid off the desk, ready to lose it completely.

Then she stopped herself. She took a deep breath. Wait a second. Gina didn't exactly have a lock on honesty, nor were any of her motivations regarding Lindsay noble. She seemed to know too much about Lindsay. She could have found out about Denver's swimming somewhere too and easily could have made the whole thing up about being with him just to rock the boat further.

Never mind that it worked like a charm.

But sometimes Lindsay's instinct for trusting no one really did save her ass. She certainly didn't trust Gina. And, she knew in a rush of warmth, she certainly did trust Denver.

"Thanks for the recommendation." She made sure her voice sounded calm and unconcerned. "If you say he's good, he must be."

Gina's silence made her feel a tiny bit better. Score one for Lindsay. Finally.

"So, Gina, I imagine you've called to talk money."

"My favorite topic."

"I can't afford to give you any more."

"Maybe not now but if your contact comes through with cash for the bar renovation, you'll be swimming in it. For the sake of our friendship, I won't keep asking for raises but I really think I underpriced myself at the beginning."

"Right." Lindsay sank wearily into a chair, starting to get chilly in what had been a very hot office only a few minutes before. Friendship? This was the kind of friend Lindsay had always had. A few weeks ago— even a few days ago she would have found it easier to accept this situation as just one of those things she'd come to expect. Now she wanted to be like her half sisters and laugh at misfortune, be like Denver and share everything that bothered her, confident she'd be understood and forgiven.

"So let's stay in touch. When you do get a definite answer from this woman, we can talk details. Oh, and I meant to tell you, I heard from our buddy Craig the other day! Of all people. He called out of the blue, saying he was in town and wanted to look me up. I told him I was still in touch with you and he said to say hi. Remember that totally hot night when the three of us did it in the—"

"Yes." She cringed. That was someone else, another woman. This Lindsay had no connection with that person anymore. "I have to go, Gina."

"Oh, sure. Great to talk to you as always. Oh, and by the way, Denver loves to be talked dirty to if he hasn't told you yet."

"I'll remember." She hung up the phone. Her fake confidence gone, she felt more miserable and exhausted than she'd ever felt in all her miserable, exhausting life. But one thing was sure. One thing. She would survive this. She would get herself out of it somehow. And whether she and Denver worked out, and whether or not she ever felt comfortable in the company of her sisters, what they'd all brought to her had already changed her, given her something higher to shoot for.

From now on, she'd settle for nothing less.

DENVER WAITED, STATUE-STILL, in the shadowy corner of the bar until Lindsay had gone upstairs. Oldest trick in the book. After he'd left her office, he'd pretended also to leave the bar by opening and closing the door. Then he'd stayed behind to eavesdrop on her conversation.

Noble? No. Even now he felt slightly sick at what he'd decided to do.

But the conversation with Brooke about pushing Lindsay had only been the first step in his determination to find out once and for all what was going on. The sight of her face when the phone had rung took him the rest of the way.

She was terrified. Worse, instinct told him she was not just terrified he'd find out who the caller was but terrified of the caller.

His relief that the caller wasn't a man had been short-lived. Yes, his ego was pleased that Brooke had read the situation correctly and he most likely didn't have competition but his main concern was for Lindsay. This woman, whoever she was, might not be threatening physically the way an abusive ex-boyfriend would be, but obviously she had a pretty unpleasant hold over Lindsay. Enough to scare one of the toughest women he'd had the pleasure to know into a near panic.

So he'd stayed in the bar. Sidled as close to her office as he dared, keeping absolutely silent and out of the light and he'd listened. The caller was someone named Gina. Someone Lindsay was paying. Someone who wanted more money than she was getting.

His first thought was that the bar was bankrupt and some creditor was harassing her. Maybe she was looking for investors to save the bar, not improve it?

Except he'd seen the books, he knew the bar had been handed over to Lindsay in solid financial shape. He knew their suppliers were paid on time. If creditors

were after her badly enough to scare her, word would
get around, deliveries would stop or drivers would
demand money up front. He couldn't believe Lindsay
would fake profits when there weren't any.

So what was it then? Had she borrowed personal
money and couldn't pay it back? He shuddered, thinking
of loan sharks, mob connections. But if that was the case
why would she be looking to expand the bar? Lindsay
was a shrewd business woman and the bar was doing
well. If she had debts, she'd pay those down, especially
if someone wanted the money badly enough to scare her.

None of it made sense unless…

Blackmail? He shook his head. Over what? She held
her private life close. But come on, blackmail was the
stuff of TV movies.

So what else? What other explanation? No one he
knew named Gina was connected with the bar. Lindsay
had never mentioned her, not that she ever mentioned
anything about her personal life.

Who was Gina?

He counted to one hundred in the darkness, then
walked toward her office, dark now since she'd turned
off the light when she'd left. If he turned it back on, she
might notice the glow upstairs or out on the sidewalk if
she happened to glance out her window. He'd grab a
flashlight from the kitchen.

Back with flashlight in hand, still uneasy about intruding on her privacy like this, he went quickly through her
files, most of which were familiar to him, none of which
she'd denied him access to. Everything looked normal.

He booted up her computer, scanned her financial software for evidence of payment to anyone named Gina, did a file search for any document mentioning her.

Nothing. So did she skim cash out of the profits and hand it over? Why? How?

There had to be some record somewhere. Someone as meticulous as Lindsay wouldn't be able to stop herself making some kind of record somewhere.

But then she wouldn't be so careless as to leave it lying around for anyone to find. So where would it be? In a hidden computer file? A hidden paper file? Locked away somewhere? He had master keys to the bar but she wasn't likely to slip up and give him the means to unlock anything she didn't want him to find.

Maybe the evidence wasn't even here. It could be upstairs, it could be…anywhere. Odds were he'd run out of time before he found it.

His cell phone vibrated in his pocket and he yanked it out. Damn. If it was Lindsay he couldn't answer it. But if it was Lindsay he'd have to. How often did she reach out to him when she was upset? His hope rose. This would be the first.

It wasn't Lindsay. He waited until the icon showed up indicating he had voice mail then punched in the code to listen. His surgeon friend Alec, saying hello, and long time no see and he'd heard from Jack that Denver was in town and between jobs. He had an opening in his practice and wondered if Denver would like to get together soon to talk. Then he left his number, slowly and distinctly, and hung up.

Denver shoved his phone back into his pocket and resumed his search. Alec was a good friend and a damn fine doctor, who obviously remembered Denver's night owl habits to be calling so late. They shared philosophies on the shortcomings of the profession, on the kind of surgery they cared about most, on the way to treat the whole patient, not just the problem. He was honest, hardworking, even-tempered. His patients adored him. A woman whose baby's cleft palate he'd corrected brought him cookies every other week for a year.

The offer would be a good one. It would promise him a better life than being on his hands and knees in a bar office prying into the life of a woman who didn't want him to know about it. Denver was a doctor. Not a P.I.

Alec's call was a timely hint that he should go back to being one.

Just now when he'd been kissing Lindsay, she'd responded in a way she never had before. Her whole demeanor that evening had been more open to him, more receptive, as if she'd finally decided to allow herself to feel what she felt. But that kissing…

He'd felt it in his heart, a slow steady melt that he didn't have to be a psychologist to know was serious, and didn't have to be a mind reader to know she was feeling too.

Then she'd withdrawn. Again. Acted as if the hot sex between them was electric and thrilling merely for the erotic value. And when the phone rang and he gave her every chance to confide in him, once again, the deep freeze.

Maybe distance would be good for them, maybe getting away from the constant sexual attraction that clouded their every interaction would help them see more clearly whether what lay between them had substance. Or not.

If nothing else, he'd be able to keep a firmer grip on his sanity than her hot-cold transformations allowed him now. He knew she acted out of genuine emotion, that she had old pain and patterns to work through, that she wasn't playing games with him. Still, a guy could only take so much.

Half an hour later, every possible file in the computer and every possible inch of her office searched, he'd found nothing. Where else could he look? What else could he do?

Two choices popped into his head. One, butt out. Call Alec back, quit the bar and move on, away from Lindsay and her problems, which she was so determined to shoulder without him.

But he'd agreed with Brooke that Lindsay needed a push. After that one confession the previous week and the way she'd been with him tonight leading up to the kiss, he couldn't withdraw his net from under her. Not now.

Which left him with only one choice: to pick an appropriate place and time to be alone with Lindsay and confront her with what he'd overheard tonight.

10

"WANT TO TAKE A WALK?"

Lindsay raised her head from the inventory report she was studying. Huh? Had she heard Denver correctly? "A walk?"

"Yeah, put one foot in front of the other with the intention of moving forward, preferably outside."

"When?" She couldn't leave now. The bar was—

"Now, Lindsay."

"But…"

She stopped herself. Last time she'd pushed him away, when she'd been on the phone with Gina, he'd not only gone, he'd kept going. If she kept sending him away eventually he'd go for good. She had finally admitted to herself that she really did not want him gone. Most likely the walk was an excuse to angle for an apology or an explanation of the phone call last night. The former she owed him and had no problem delivering. The latter…

"Lindsay, for crying out loud. It's eleven o'clock, the bar is practically empty and Justin is on top of things. Our cells will be on, we won't go far, and…" He grinned and pointed to the window. "It's snowing."

"Really?" She peered at the window of her office, half covered by a filing cabinet. Sure enough, clumps of flakes were floating down between her building and the one next door. "Wow. This time of year I'd rather be reminded we're heading toward beach weather, but—"

"Beach weather? In Massachusetts? In February?"

"Hey." She shot him an exasperated look. "You can't stop a girl from dreaming."

"I wouldn't dare try. So how about it? You and me and a cold sidewalk?"

"Hmm." She frowned down at the paper in front of her. "Going over inventory versus a romantic late night walk in the snow with the hottest man I know…gosh, that's a tough one."

He made a rude noise and tossed over her coat. "C'mon."

"Okay, okay." She stood and put it on. "If the bar catches fire, it's all your fault."

"Uh-huh." He escorted her through the door. "What do you do when there's nothing to worry about, make stuff up?"

"Ha. Ha." She turned toward the bar. "Justin, we're—"

"I know, boss lady, off for a nighttime stroll." He winked and spun a glass. "Have fun. Everything's under control here."

"He knew?" She glared up at Denver. "You taking me for granted?"

His chuckle was drier than she expected. "Trust me, not a chance."

"Good." They moved toward the door, Lindsay pulling on her gloves, then stepped out onto Beaumont Street into air surprisingly mild and utterly still. Her favorite kind of snow, large flakes falling slowly and silently in the darkness, glowing brightly under the streetlights, retreating to gray in the shadows. Already the sidewalks were lightly covered.

"It's pretty." She spoke not only the truth, but also to fill the silence, which seemed suddenly awkward. Denver had come in to work that afternoon jovial and friendly, as if nothing had happened the previous night, as if she hadn't ordered him out of the room while they were practically still joined so she could talk to Gina privately.

In turn she'd acted as if Gina hadn't said a word about getting sexual with Denver. Even if Gina was telling the truth about Denver, what he'd done before he got involved with Lindsay was none of her business. God knew she hadn't come to him a virgin. Maybe at some point, at the right time, she'd ask. Maybe not. Doubtless Denver had no idea who Gina really was or how she was connected to Lindsay. Nor would he give away any of her secrets about the bar.

She really hoped, now that they were out here with the city looking so beautiful and the snow falling so peacefully, that he wasn't going to bring up yesterday's—

"About last night, Lindsay. I think we still have some things to talk about."

Right on cue. Of course. "Is that why you lured me out here with promises of romance?"

"I don't think I promised you that."

A heavy snowflake landed on her eyelash; she blinked rapidly to fling it off, but it melted into a cold drip that rolled down her cheek. "No. I guess you didn't."

"Last night I stayed in the bar while you were on the phone."

"What?" She turned to look at him. At the sight of his serious expression, caught between shadow and light, her heart started pounding even though the meaning of his words had yet to penetrate. "What do you mean?"

"I didn't leave the bar. I stayed and listened to your phone call."

Lindsay stopped walking, struggling to make sense of what he was saying. "But I heard you leave."

"A trick. I opened the door and closed it again. I stayed inside."

"What?" Her mind finally got it, started spinning furiously. What had she said? What had he heard? How could he *do* this? Just when she'd decided she could trust him.

He turned toward her, his face grim. "I won't say you left me no choice because that's a ridiculous clichéd excuse."

"No kidding."

"But I will say that subterfuge felt like the only thing I hadn't tried."

"In order to invade my personal life where you don't belong?"

"I don't?"

She waved her hands impatiently but the barb had hit. "Not in that particular matter, no."

"Why?"

"Because it's personal."

"Not when the mere sound of someone's voice sends you into a panic, Lindsay. Then it spills over into my business too."

"I don't see how."

"That's how relationships work."

"Who said we—" She cut off the juvenile retort, probably not in time. She was hurt, and scared and couldn't let herself retreat into anger to deal with either emotion. Even if he deserved it.

"Lindsay." His voice was deadly serious, quiet in the wide outdoors made intimate by the snow. "Did you borrow money you can't pay back?"

"No." She took a quick step away from him.

"Because I can help you."

"No."

He turned his head away; she got the feeling he was counting to ten. "Is that all you're going to say? No. No. No?"

"Yes."

"Ha. Gotcha."

She shut her eyes. "You had no right to—"

"I know. You can spare me the lecture. Believe me, I know." He closed the space she'd taken pains to put between them, resting his hands on her shoulders. She didn't resist though she thought she should. Hell, she *should* punch him in the nose. "I did not enjoy what I did. You should have seen your face when the phone rang, Lindsay. You looked terrified. I thought…"

He pressed his lips together, looking so angry and helpless, she softened.

"Thought what?"

"After what you told me in your apartment, I thought the caller might be some old boyfriend threatening to hurt you. I couldn't stand that. I needed to know."

Lindsay drew in a deep breath, watching the agony in his face. She hated what he'd done, hated his betrayal. But in the face of so much pain on her behalf, a lot of which she'd put him through, she could no longer summon enough outrage to push him away—ironically the one time he probably deserved it.

He'd thought someone was going to hurt her. He'd wanted to protect her. And he'd stepped outside of what she knew was a strong moral boundary to make sure she was going to stay safe. Powerful stuff.

The last person who swore she was protecting Lindsay, that she had her best interests at heart, was Gina. After Lindsay had shoved Ty to his death, Gina had taken her in. She'd coached her through interviews with police, fed her and helped her recover from the shock and grief even though Gina had lost a friend in Ty too. Sometimes Lindsay had suspected a lot more than a friend though she'd never bothered looking for proof.

At the time Lindsay had thought Gina's behavior was the epitome of friendship. Only when Gina had considered her sufficiently past the trauma to propose they start what amounted to a prostitution business together, maybe with a side of drug dealing, had Lindsay realized Gina didn't see her as a friend but a business investment.

How little things changed.

If Ty's death had gone a long way toward scaring Lindsay straight, Gina's proposition had done the rest.

But this man facing her here in the peaceful snowy street was not asking—nor would he ask, she was sure of it—for anything more than the chance to be closer, to make her life better. She didn't like his methods, would stand up to him and scream if he tried playing dirty again, but she owed him that chance. Like it or not, she had strong feelings for him, and was starting to lean on him and trust him more than she'd ever trusted or leaned on anyone.

"It's not an old boyfriend."

"Unless his name was Gina, I'd guessed that." His brows drew down; his lips bunched. "I can't keep doing this, Lindsay."

Panic squeezed her insides. "Doing what?"

"Begging. Pleading. Sneaking. Manipulating. I'm not insisting you let me in on every secret you have. I'm not controlling like that. You have a total right to your privacy however involved we get. I also don't want a relationship with just half of you. Whatever is going on right now is obviously consuming you. I want you to be worry-free so that the only thing consuming you is me."

She sent him a slow wry smile. "An ultimatum in sheep's clothing?"

"You drive me crazier than any woman ever has and introduced me to depths of masochism I didn't know I was capable of." He said this with such intensity she nearly stopped breathing. "I have no idea why I haven't walked away. God knows I've told myself many times I should."

"But now you're ready to? This is an ultimatum, Denver?"

He sighed and tipped his face up. She raised hers too and watched the snowflakes fall and land like sharp, cold kisses on her skin.

"Yeah. It is, Lindsay. I need something settled here. One way or the other."

She nodded, still staring up into the sky, her tension building. She didn't like ultimatums and she didn't want to have to respond to one. But if she followed her immediate prideful instinct and told him to get lost…he'd be gone. And Gina would have had the power not only to destroy Lindsay's inner peace and her profit margins, but her shot at happiness as well.

That was the kind of ultimatum she should be fighting. Not this one.

"We should get back to the bar, Denver."

"That's your answer?"

"No." She lowered her head. "But we should get back."

"Right." He turned grimly away, then stopped and offered his hand. With his heart on the line, with no clear answer and rejection possible, he still took the time to reach out to her. Would she ever meet anyone this wonderful again? She pulled off her glove, wanting skin-to-skin contact, then took his hand and squeezed his fingers.

He squeezed hers back. "Come swimming after work?"

"I was just about to invite you up to my place. So we can talk."

"Talk?" He shot her a look of mock astonishment. "Did you, Lindsay Beckham, just say you want to *talk?*"

"Okay, okay. Point taken. Do you?"

"Yes. I want to talk. And then depending on what you say I'm either going to bend you over a chair and punish you or lay you on the bed and make love to you and promise I'll be there for you no matter what *even though…*" He lifted his free hand to stop any protest. "Even though I know you can take care of yourself."

She found herself smiling. "Damn right."

He laughed, swung their arms, then curved them so hers twisted behind her back and she came up flush against him. Then he bent his head and kissed her, his lips somehow warm in spite of the chill. She kissed him back, not caring that Chassy was within sight, not caring about anything but the crazy, delicious paradox that he cared enough about having all of her to leave if he couldn't.

BY THE TIME SHE AND DENVER reached her apartment, Lindsay was exhausted. After they returned from their walk, the bar had filled suddenly and unexpectedly with Celtic basketball fans celebrating a victory over their rivals, the L.A. Lakers. The staff, who'd been enjoying a lazy evening, had to shoot into overdrive, pouring out alarming quantities of beer and hauling out tray after tray of appetizers.

Ahhh, Boston sports fans…

"I thought they'd never leave." She dragged the elastic out of her sagging ponytail. Her hair probably smelled of the deep fryer and alcohol fumes.

"Business is business."

"True." She wrinkled her nose, surprised at how comfortable she felt having him in her home. "I could use a shower. How about you?"

"Definitely."

"Want to go first?"

He shook his head, smiling wickedly. "How about you start. I'll join you."

"Okay." Lindsay stepped away from him, backwards, for a few steps, smiling, enjoying the hungry look on his face. Then she turned and went through her bedroom into her bathroom. She stepped in the shower, watching, waiting, closed her eyes, hoping he'd slip in and surprise her.

She lathered up her hair. Rinsed. Opened her eyes and peeked through the curtain toward the bathroom door for his silhouette. Nothing. She scrubbed her body. Rinsed. Still nothing. Where was he?

"Denver?"

"Mmm." He sounded like he was right outside the shower.

She pulled the curtain back farther from where it gaped already. He was naked. Watching her. With a huge…welcome. "I didn't see you. How long have you been standing there?"

"Long enough to qualify me as a voyeur pervert."

She looked down and nonchalantly raised an eyebrow,

though the sight of his thick beautiful erection made her whole body hungry. "Apparently."

"Actually it was perversion in the name of science."

"Really."

"I wanted to see if I could come just watching you."

"And?"

"Close. Cigar another time."

She laughed and dragged the curtain open farther. All the tension and misery of earlier tonight, of the last few days, weeks and months vanished when she was with him like this. When he wasn't fixating on her troubles, he created a bubble of joy and security all around her. It was similar to what she sensed her half sisters felt with each other and which she'd been drawn to in their company over and over again. That sense of safety and peace was what had attracted her to Denver initially even before she started to trust that it might be real. He seemed so easy with the world, so able to make her laugh when she most needed to relax. "Come in, Denver."

"Don't need to invite me twice." He stepped into the tub, dominating the small space with his big body. She helped him shampoo and wash, touching him lingeringly everywhere she wanted, which was everywhere, getting more and more aroused while he showed no signs of drooping himself.

Neither did he show any signs that he was naked in the shower with her for any other purpose except to get clean. For some odd reason that was comforting. And damned exciting.

They shared a towel, one of the huge bath sheets

Lindsay had indulged in—one of her very few indulgences—rubbing each other's bodies, sometimes rubbing together, but still, neither of them made any move to take their closeness further. The anticipation was torture. The only kind of torture she enjoyed.

"Come on." He took her hand, led her out of the bathroom and into the bedroom.

He turned out the lights as she turned down the sheets. They burrowed in together, naked clean bodies on cool clean cotton under the thick down comforter.

There couldn't be anything in the universe more wonderful than this.

Except the silence stretched expectantly and she realized he was more tense than he'd let on, waiting for her answer. She had to tell him what was going on with Gina or he'd give up on her.

It wasn't a choice, not really. But how and where could she start? See, Denver, I killed my last boyfriend, so you really shouldn't piss me off…

She could start by admitting she didn't know where to start. That was something. At least she'd be talking. "I don't know how to do this, Denver."

"Do what?"

"How to tell you what you want to know."

"Do you want to tell me?"

"Yes."

"Just because I threatened to leave?"

She inhaled, long and slow, blew it out likewise, and admitted a truth she'd probably known for a while. "No. Not entirely."

He turned toward her, a dark male shadow against the white cotton, and kissed her over and over, lips soft and possessive, arms wrapping tightly around her. She pushed against him, straddled her leg over his hip to bring them into sexual contact. He resisted, pushed her leg gently back down and stroked her body and her hair, slow, firm caresses that made her feel completely encircled by his warmth.

Her arousal leveled; she surrendered to the sweet agony of holding back. She immersed herself in kissing him, aware of the slight grind of his stubbled chin, the varying pressure and position of his lips, the thick, soft strands of his hair, the solid muscle of his torso against her. Slowly her heart swelled, painfully, exquisitely, until the truth was again too obvious to ignore. She loved him, and would never love anyone again in quite this way. The rest of the world gradually disappeared, faded in importance, then faded altogether. She loved him. There was no other explanation possible. And the realization brought no panic, only joy and overpowering awe.

Finally, he stopped kissing her, then bent his head slightly so their foreheads touched and she could feel his breath.

"I had a girlfriend in high school." He spoke in barely above a whisper. "Her name was Jenna. She was beautiful, looked a little like you, but less exotic, more girl-next-door cute."

"Exotic?" She snorted. "Be serious."

"This is my story, be quiet."

She grinned, she couldn't help it. "Go on."

"I loved her with all my teenaged heart. She was my first. I was hers. I asked her to marry me when I was nineteen and she said yes."

Jealousy pierced her so intensely she nearly gasped with it. *Calm down, Lindsay. This was over a decade ago.* "You married her?"

"No."

She exhaled her relief and he chuckled. "That bothered you?"

Denial was her automatic response. She bit it back. "Yes."

"Just listen. About six months after we were engaged, she was in an accident. A speeder ran a red light, clipped her car and sent her into a light pole." His voice was calm. "She survived but with several deep and damaging cuts on her face."

"Oh God. How horrible." Jealousy disappeared into shame. "The poor woman."

"She had surgery but the scars were still visible. She became obsessed, sure she was no longer attractive or desirable. Nothing I said or did could convince her that my feelings hadn't changed. She pushed me away until I finally gave up. And I left."

Lindsay didn't breathe. How close had she come to doing the exact same thing? This Jenna person had been a fool. Lucky for Lindsay. "That must have been hell."

"It was. But it changed my life in two important ways. One, it convinced me to go into plastic surgery instead of oncology. Because even though she couldn't see it, the way they'd put her back together inspired me."

"And two?"

"Two, it taught me something important about love."

She swallowed, hardly daring to hope. "Which is?"

"You can't really love someone until you've seen them at their worst and love them in spite of it. And you don't know how you'll function as a couple until you've been through crap together and survived it. After Jenna I stopped believing in the giddy first rush of feelings. I didn't get serious about anyone for a long time." He moved his hand under her chin, tipped her mouth up and kissed her so sweetly she felt tears come into her eyes. "Until now."

The tears spilled over, there was no way she could stay strong enough to resist them now. "Thank you."

An utterly inane thing to say.

"Yeah, don't mention it." He responded as if she'd thanked him for opening a door, and she laughed. Again. He knew she was overwhelmed and had given her a break from the intensity.

Then silence. Nearly unbearable. It was her turn and she felt some of the panic she'd avoided before. "Denver, I know I'm supposed to—"

"Shh."

He rolled her to her back, proceeded to stroke and kiss every inch of her body until her tension was replaced by the tension of sexual excitement.

They'd been together before, but this felt like the first time. She felt clean, not only in her body and in her bed, but in her heart. And when he entered her, she wrapped her arms around his shoulders and wished the light were on so she could see his face, so she could watch his eyes and connect with him the way their bodies were connected.

His rhythm was easy, leisurely flow instead of an urgent rush toward explosion. In. And out. In. And out. Filling her perfectly, teasing her clitoris, keeping her on the edge of arousal.

And then suddenly, at the most unlikely time, in the middle of this beautifully languid erotic journey, she wanted to tell him. Everything. Pour it out and clean her soul along with everything else.

"Denver."

"Mmm." He kissed each corner of her mouth.

"I want…I have to tell you."

"Should I stop?" His voice was light, and it made her relax.

"No." It would be easier this way with the incredible tenderness between them.

She pressed her cheek to his and told him. About her childhood. About leaving home at seventeen. About the drugs. About the indiscriminate, uninhibited sex. About Ty, his possessiveness that had felt like love, but had turned into control and abuse. About their last fight and his taunts about keeping her with him always, meaning he'd never, ever allow her to leave his control. About how he'd come at her with that cruel, familiar sneer on his face, and in a blind alcohol-fueled rage she'd shoved him back, away from her with all her strength, how he'd fought back and she'd pushed, kicked, punched, wanting only to get him off her, away from her, out of her life. About his stumbling, her final push, his fall, about the horror of his death, about Gina taking her in, and what Gina had in mind for their future. About Lindsay turning her life around. And…finally, in a voice that choked even more painfully, about Gina showing up again and charging for her silence.

"My God." He stopped moving; his voice was low with horror. "My God, Lindsay."

Lindsay squeezed her eyes shut, the fear of rejection painful already. How could he fail to be repulsed by the story? She'd been repulsed telling it. More than she had been living it.

"How the hell have you been able to bear all that by yourself?"

She opened her eyes. "What?"

"Why didn't you tell someone? Why didn't you tell me this before? I could have helped you, I could have—" He took in a sharp breath, blew it out slowly. "I'm sorry. I know how hard that must have been. Thank you for telling me. I'm glad you did."

"Me too." She was surprised to find the words were absolutely true. Even if he'd rejected her, even if he'd freaked out, the crushing weight was so much lessened now. Just for having told someone.

She smiled. No. Of course not. For having told *him*.

"I'm going to help you, Lindsay." He started moving again, his whisper intensified by the darkness. "She's not going to win this."

"Denver…"

"What is it?" He paused in his rhythm, and then as

if he couldn't bear to stop, he groaned and moved again, faster, more urgently.

She'd been going to say no, that she'd handle this herself, that she always handled everything herself and always would.

But she suddenly realized that wasn't true. Or at least, that she no longer wanted it to be true.

"Make love to me." She murmured the words, knowing she was really telling him she loved him, unable to say that, not quite yet. "Make it all go away, make me come so hard that everything…everything goes away."

He groaned again, dug his hands under her hips to gain more control.

"Everything?"

She took his head in her hands, brought his mouth down to hers. "Everything…except you."

11

LINDSAY HAD BEEN DREAMING about Ty. In her dream
Denver had again invited her swimming, and this time
she'd decided to go. She'd walked there, her dream
strides magically eating up the miles between South
Boston and Brookline, anticipating his excited reaction
when she showed up. At his neighbors' house, a
mansion in her dream, Denver was in the middle of the
enormous pool, treading water, staring at her blankly,
and she'd felt self-conscious taking off her clothes—
down to the lingerie she'd bought with her half sisters.
He'd made no move to come close and she'd had to
swim toward him. The closer she swam, the farther
away he seemed from her until in a strange blurred,
splashing rush, as though her feet had sprouted flippers,
she reached him. Finally. She'd smiled into his face,
only to see Denver's warm brown eyes morph disturb-
ingly into Ty's hot blue ones, Denver's jaw loosen and
descend into Ty's jowls, his chin sharpen, his hair
lighten and curl. Ty, with his lip half lifted the way he'd
looked when he was angry and feeling violent, lacing
his fingers, wrapping his hands over the top of her head,

pushing her under. She writhed, shoved, wrestled. He let her up for a huge openmouthed gasping breath only to hold her under again.

She woke, struggling for air, then realized she'd been holding her breath in her sleep.

"Lindsay. It's okay. You're awake now. It's okay." Denver's voice, Denver's hand on her shoulder. Ty was gone. Ty was dead. She was safe. With Denver. Safe.

"Yes. Sorry. I'm awake." She blinked, pulling herself out of the thick sleep-fog, staring at the window opposite her bed. The light coming in around the edges of the shades was gray and dull like the mood in her head.

"Bad dream?"

"Yes." She still couldn't get her breathing to settle down.

"It's over. Everything's going to get better now. I'm going to help you through all the crap you've been dealing with." He whispered endearments, stroking up from her shoulder to her hair. She tried not to flinch, remembering the huge hands pushing her under in her dream.

"I'm fine." Lindsay sat up, not wanting to be touched anymore, not wanting him so close even though he had nothing to do with Ty or the part of her subconscious that made her dream she was being drowned. But until she shook off the remnants of this strange mood, she needed space. "Be right back."

She slid off the bed and trudged into the bathroom where she splashed cold water on her face, hating the way her dreams affected her so powerfully. After her confession last night, she should have woken up happy, contented, freed from the solitude of her burden, able to burrow in next to Denver and enjoy the closeness.

Her face in the mirror looked back, dripping and hunted. Damn Ty. His final words were even more haunting now. Maybe he was right that he'd never let her go, even after death.

The thought chased her out of the bathroom and nearly smack into Denver, who was waiting to come in. She reared back, smiling apologetically.

"It's only me." He grinned, looking warm and tall and solid, standing with his hair all rumpled and bed-headed. "Go back to bed, I'll join you in a second."

She nodded dumbly, returned to the bedroom and slipped between the still-warm sheets, pulling the comforter over her, staring at the ceiling, at a gray cobweb in the corner and next to it, a jagged crack in the paint. Slowly the fog cleared from her mind but her feeling of dread lingered, as if she were back in the pool on a day turned sunny and fine, but still able to sense threatening shadows darting underneath her.

"Back to reality?" Powerfully naked, completely at ease in his bare skin, Denver strolled into the room, bounced into bed under the covers, reached for her. His world was always sunny and fine. What did he know about her black shadows? He seemed so sure he could banish them.

"Yes, back to reality." She reached and mischievously brushed unruly hair off his forehead. "Nice style."

"You think? I call it The Morning After."

"Very chic."

He lifted a lock of her heavy straight hair. "Your hair wouldn't muss in a tornado."

"No kidding." She pushed her hand through the strands she'd always wanted to replace with a sexy tousled mane like Katie's.

"It fits the rest of you. I can see you at the hour of the apocalypse, sitting at your desk among screaming panicked hordes, calmly making sure your paperwork is in shape."

"One must *always* have the paperwork in shape."

"But, of course." His smile turned serious. "I hope you let yourself freak out to me once in a while, Lindsay."

"Didn't I do that last night?" She grinned, wanting to keep things light between them, still spooked by her dream. "How many women have men begging them to be *more* emotional?"

"One at least." He launched himself unexpectedly over her, supporting himself on his elbows, ready to lower himself on board. She squealed, but not with any real fear. This was Denver. "Right now I want *you* to beg *me*."

"Oh?" Her fingers followed the muscled curves of his arms up to his shoulders and around to the back of his neck. "What could I *possibly* want to beg *you* for?"

"You know…" He moved his eyebrows suggestively.

She shrugged, all affected innocence. "I really have no idea."

"None?"

"Nope." She poked his shoulder playfully. "Tell me. What am I supposed to beg you for?"

"A hot 'n healthy serving of man meat, baybee."

Lindsay's laughter burst out of her, startling away the black shadows and propelling her into his sunny and fine day. *"Man meat?"*

"At your service." He lowered his body on top of hers, kissed her cheeks, her forehead, her nose while she vainly tried to stop snorting and snickering. Then slow and warm, he kissed the corners of her mouth, moving his hips suggestively over hers, and her urge to giggle fled as quickly as the shadows.

"I don't think I'll ever stop wanting you with me, Lindsay."

She basked in his words, ignoring their similarity to Ty's final taunt. Would she ever stop wanting Denver? It seemed impossible.

"We'll work out what to do about Gina." He rolled to the side and laid his palm possessively on her abdomen. "Joey might be able to help with legal advice. When are you going to see her again?"

"I don't know." She shifted restlessly; her stomach gurgling against his fingers. She didn't want to think about this right now. She wanted sunny and fine, sexy and fun.

"The Winfields have to have connections in law enforcement. I can ask Brooke. Her grandfather Henry is just the type to have a judge or two in his pocket. District attorney would be even better."

"I don't want the Winfields involved."

"Not even your sisters?"

"Half sisters." She turned to him, laid her hand on his chest. "Not even them."

He ran an impatient hand through his hair. "You

can't still insist on handling this yourself. Are you even going to let *me* help you?"

"I don't know." She took her hand away from his chest, breaking the contact, desperation rising in her throat. "I haven't made these decisions. I only just told you last night."

"But you must have thought about it. You've lived with this threat for months. You must have worked out some solutions."

She said nothing. What could she say except that she wasn't him. She didn't think or act like him. Hadn't done the things he obviously assumed any normal human would do.

"There has to be some way to stop her and keep you safe, Lindsay. I don't have any expertise in that area and you don't either. We're going to need help."

She sat up, hugged her knees, aware she probably looked like a petulant child. This was too much; he was pushing too hard, too soon. "I don't want anybody's help. It's too risky. There's too much at stake."

"Come on." He lifted his hand, resting it on the mattress's empty space between them. "You can't seriously expect a jury would convict you. I doubt the D.A. would even press charges."

She shook her head. "You don't understand."

"Okay." Denver turned his palm up to her. "What don't I understand?"

"I'm not like you. My past isn't like yours. My pedigree isn't like yours. People like me don't get pats on the back and a free ride out of the justice system."

He made a sound of frustration. "Why are you so anxious to condemn yourself? Why can't you forgive yourself when everyone else has?"

"I doubt Ty would."

"Ty is dead. And from what you told me, I won't say he deserved it but I doubt he'd be surprised at what you did."

"You didn't know him."

"Thank God for that." He laughed bitterly. "If I had known him, he would have ended up the same way he is now only much sooner. And I would have a lot less of a defense than you do."

Lindsay tried to breathe past the lump in her throat, the acid churning in her stomach. She'd spent so long convincing herself that her actions since Gina showed up again had been the right ones to take that she found his challenge extremely unsettling. She couldn't seem to listen and comprehend. He only made her want to hunker down and turn stubbornly resistant. What was right? She couldn't tell. Not now, not with him on the attack. She was all fight or flight and no logic.

Denver glanced suddenly at the clock by her bed, slid to the edge of the mattress and stood. "I didn't realize it was so late. I have to get back to my apartment, shower and shave and get dressed. I'm meeting a friend for an early lunch downtown."

Lindsay nodded. For some reason the dread that started with her nightmare returned to take hold in the pit of her stomach. Because he had to go? Was she already getting that dependent on him? "What friend?"

He glanced at her in a way that made the dread worse, then reached for his pants. "Alec Swanson. I knew him in medical school at Brown. He's one of the best plastic surgeons I know. He's in town and called me when he found out I was here too. His practice needs a new partner."

Lindsay reached for the comforter that had covered them all night, gathering its warmth around her. "He wants you to work with him."

"We're going to discuss it."

She nodded, the black shadows circling again. "That sounds perfect for you."

Denver pulled his shirt over his head and down over his beautiful chest "It would be a good move. But today all we're going to do is talk. And even if I do go, I'm not leaving you, Lindsay, just your employment."

"Right. I know." She knew all too well what would happen.

"Which means…" He winked at her. "I wouldn't be able to slap you with a sexual harassment lawsuit anymore."

Her brows went up. Keep it cheery. Keep it light. "Excuse me, I believe that's my suit to make against you."

"Oh yeah?" He lunged onto the bed, knocking her gently onto her back. Again she felt no fear…but the dread was stronger still. He kissed her lingeringly. She resisted the urge to wrap her arms around his neck and pull him too close for him to be able to go. "I wish we had time for more. I'll call you after lunch. And I'll see you tonight."

"You're not on the schedule tonight."

"So I'm not." He grinned and slid off the bed. "I'll put in some unpaid overtime. How's about that?"

"As long as you never mention the phrase hot 'n healthy man meat ever again."

"It's a deal." He went back toward the bed, affectionately squeezed her foot with his warm, big hands. "I'm sorry to have to leave so suddenly."

"No problem." She spoke abruptly, sat up and shoved herself off the bed. Then she walked him to her front door, kissed him and watched as he went down the stairs, turning to wave at the bottom before he disappeared out onto Beaumont Street.

The dark shadows took over completely plunging her into despair. He was going to leave. Men always left. Either physically or emotionally, like Ty, by turning into someone she no longer recognized.

Denver would go back to his old life, his respectable upscale doctor's life where he belonged. It wouldn't take long for him to forget his wild little ride with a bar owner from the wrong side of the tracks. For all she knew, once the novelty wore off, her half sisters would drift away too, their relationship a victim of their differences. And she'd be left at the mercy of a blackmailer, having come as close to real love and real family as she'd ever been before. How typical, to find herself once again in danger of having all the carefully chosen pieces of her life fall completely apart.

DENVER SHOOK HANDS WITH Alec, then he strode down Boylston Street toward his car. He'd miraculously found a spot to park near where they'd eaten lunch. Clearly some things were meant to be. Even the sun had broken through the February gloom and warmed the air with the suggestion of spring.

Lunch had been invigorating. Alec was as friendly and stimulating and funny as always, and their conversation flowed effortlessly as if they'd only seen each other a week before instead of several years. Alec's practice was thriving, his emphasis and philosophy were still extremely close to what Denver was looking for. It seemed almost too good to be true to have an opportunity like this fall into his lap. Alec had offered him a chance to come in and look around and see what he thought but Denver already had a very good feeling that this partnership would become a reality.

He jogged the last few yards to his car, pumped up and feeling better than he'd felt in a long, long time, ready to welcome a new beginning. It was definitely time he got off his ass and got his act together. Now with a real relationship starting with Lindsay, and the opportunity to resume a career he loved by practicing the way he needed to practice, he felt as if all the pieces of his life were falling back into place.

At the same time…

He'd seen Lindsay's face when he told her he was thinking about leaving Chassy and getting on with his life. She would never admit it but he suspected she'd need a lot more reassurance that his move away from the bar by no means encompassed a move away from her. On the contrary. With his new job he'd be in a much better position to offer her a future because he'd know exactly what and where that future would be. His only concern was that the early months of his new practice would be all consuming so he'd need to get her trouble with this Gina person solved as soon as possible. He understood Lindsay's resistance and her fears, but in a situation as dangerous as hers, he had no patience with the sit-back-and-see-what-happens attitude, especially now that he realized how much he missed by not going forward in his own life.

His phone rang on his way into his car and he got back out to answer it in the sunshine. He checked the display, hoping it was Lindsay, suspecting it wouldn't be. She'd still be home pretending she didn't have any stake in how his lunch went. One of these days he'd have her opened up and feeling safe with him. Already he'd made progress.

"Hi, Mom."

"Is it cold there?"

Denver grinned. His mom never missed an opportunity to needle him about being stuck in frigid Boston while she and his father were basking in the heat of Greece. "Not too bad. Low forties, maybe. Cold there?"

"I'm on our veranda sipping coffee watching the Mediterranean sparkle in the sun."

"Whew, rough life. I wouldn't trade places with you for anything."

His mother laughed. "How are you, dear heart?"

He told her about his lunch with Alec knowing she'd be thrilled, and that his father would be even more thrilled because they hadn't raised their son to while his nights away in a bar now, had they.

"Well, it's about time. Your father will hit the moon. I'll tell him the second he gets home."

"From fishing?"

His mother sighed wearily. "What else? I actually called because Bob Grouper, do you remember him? I think his daughter was a year ahead of you in high school. Emily was it?"

"Yes. Emily. I remember." He rolled his eyes, completely uninterested in all the gossip his mother loved.

"He's having heart surgery. Your father and I want to be back stateside there to cheer him on and help Annabel out however we can. So we're going to be home late tomorrow, Saturday. I wanted to give you at least some warning so you'd have time to find new homes for The Swedish Bikini Team, any animals you might have adopted and of course you'll want to relocate your illegal drug business."

Denver chuckled automatically, annoyed she still treated him like a teenager who needed to rebel. At the same time his mind was spinning. He'd need to find a new place to stay. As much as he loved his parents, living with them meant he immediately regained little boy status in their eyes. If he was trying to cope with them and a new job at the same time, he'd probably go crazy.

Immediately he thought of Lindsay's spacious and comfortable apartment. Which lead to thoughts of Lindsay naked in the bed as he left her this morning.

Which led to the type of fantasies he should not be having while he was on the phone with his mother.

"I'll make sure the house is in shape, Mom. It's about time I found a place of my own anyway now that I'm most likely staying in Boston."

"Of course you're welcome to stay with us as long as you need to…"

Denver smiled. Hidden message: *but you'd be in the way and don't expect me to do your laundry.*

"I'll find my own place. Have a safe trip back, Mom. Can't wait to see you. Say hi to Dad."

Denver disconnected after receiving more of her congratulations brimming with relief that her son wasn't a shiftless bum anymore, got into his car and drove back to his parents' house in Brookline. The sight of the familiar beige colonial, a far cry from the villa they rented with the Robinsons on Mykonos, made him think about coming home. Which made him think about Lindsay. And the more he thought about Lindsay, the more moving in with her seemed like a good solution. His daily presence would erase any fears she might have of him leaving more than just his job at Chassy. And being together would allow them to continue to build their relationship more easily when he was likely to be busy starting with a new practice. Any fears she had of him moving too fast he'd keep at bay by emphasizing the situation was temporary, just until he found a place of his own, which was true. In the meantime they could get a better sense of how well they'd do together.

He suspected well. Very well. Just the idea of coming home to a place they shared, waking up with her every morning… He'd be able to take care of her in a way he suspected she'd never experienced, but probably craved on some deep level. Though he'd have a hell of a time getting her to admit that. Who didn't crave a little spoiling? Enjoying a little ease had nothing to do with weakness. He hoped to be able to teach her that. She'd taken on and fought under far too many burdens. If he could make her life easier, even if that meant nothing more than having a meal and a back rub ready for her after closing, then he'd do whatever he could to make it happen.

Denver grinned, so infatuated with the fantasy he dialed her number right in his parents' driveway, closing his eyes and turning his face to the sun.

"Hello?"

"Hi there." He smiled. Her voice made him happy and a little hard.

"Denver." She sounded wary, which he'd expected. "How was lunch?"

"Good. Great." He told her about how good it was to see Alec, how his vision for the clinic was what Denver had always wanted to do. He told her what a great opportunity it was, how excited he felt that his life was getting back on track.

"When do you start?" she asked flatly.

"He wants me as soon as possible." Denver grinned, feeling like a surprise party host, about to usher the guest of honor into an apparently empty dull room where guests and a lavish party were waiting, hidden by darkness. "I figure for the first few weeks I can get the feel for the new job and still help you at Chassy during the transition to hiring someone else."

"Sure."

"Lindsay, this is a beginning, not an end." She had that injured tone which meant she thought he was withdrawing, and suddenly he found himself apprehensive. "I just heard from my parents. They're coming back early. So it looks like I'll need a new place to stay until I can find a place of my own."

"Oh."

He sighed. He looked forward to when this beautiful, incredible woman was no longer ruled by fear. "I was hoping you'd have room for me at your place."

Silence.

"Not a good idea?"

"I...don't know."

"I thought it was pretty practical." His jaw tightened. After last night and this morning, if she retreated now... "It would just be temporary until I find a permanent place, a few weeks maximum, a lot sooner if an apartment or condo shows up right away. I can stay in your extra bedroom if you want. Most of my stuff is in storage. I can leave nonessentials at my parents' house. So I won't be taking over."

More silence.

"I know I'm springing this on you..."

"Yeah. Okay. I'll think about it."

Right. Think about it, worry about it, try to unearth

all the underlying evil that he could be planning, all the subversive, controlling manipulating moves that she should damn well know by now he wasn't capable of. Ugly fear crept into his euphoria. Weren't they ever going to get past all this? Two steps forward, three steps back? Fear he was leaving her life, fear he was moving into it too fast? So much damn fear it contradicted itself.

It was all he could do not to shout at her. *If I wait for you to think about it, it's never going to happen.* Forget it. The idea was a good one, she had to see that. He'd make it happen. "I'll be over tonight with my stuff. If you decide you don't want me there, you can kick me out."

He waited a beat for her objection. When it didn't come, he said goodbye and hung up, feeling unsettled but triumphant. He could find a place in a month, maybe less. Secretly, he hoped they got along so well that she wouldn't want him to move out. But he knew better than to mention anything permanent now.

Brooke had been right. Lindsay needed pushing out of the burning building into his net. He was fleetingly sorry for all the months he'd hung back waiting and hoping for her to come to him. Now he saw more clearly that the only way his relationship with Lindsay could move forward was if he geared himself up and shoved it there.

12

HE WAS MOVING IN. LINDSAY TRIED the concept out again in her mind, methodically taking down chairs from the tops of bar tables where she'd placed them last night so the cleaning crew could get a good shot at the floors.

Her uneasiness had only grown during the day. She'd opened herself up to him, taken that first baby step, felt proud, but vulnerable as hell. She needed time to feel steady on her feet before taking the next baby step and the next. Instead, it seemed the horizon held nothing but changes.

When Denver announced he was looking into other job possibilities that morning, she'd reacted immediately. As much as she still had hopes he wasn't like the rest—as much as she *knew* he wasn't like the rest—all men loved the chase. She couldn't count how many had pursued her, then as soon as she allowed herself to think she'd found some kind of safe harbor and started to count on them, they'd drifted away. Naturally, Denver wanted to resume his career, and this opportunity was fabulous. But she hadn't been able to tamp down her deeply rooted fear of rejection.

Ironically, one phone call later, her fear was no longer that he'd disappear from her life, but that he'd take it over. She knew she must be unbearably frustrating him with her caution. She knew she'd already forced him to use a saint's amount of patience and then some. She knew any reasonable man would have long ago given up and run. And she couldn't blame him for wanting to claim his spoils of victory by taking that yard once she'd given her inch.

But he was almost acting as though it were up to him how to handle the blackmail situation, as though he could now decide everything for her future and the bar's because they'd spent a few hours in bed together. Now this. Moving into her apartment tonight, barely giving her time to adjust to the idea, to offer objection.

She put a chair down and sank into it, aware her apprehension was making her put too much of the blame on Denver. She could have just said no. But she'd immediately been struck by her usual combination of joy and fear. Joy at the thought of having him around combined with relief that he really wasn't planning to leave more than the bar, and yet perversely, fear of the same. She couldn't, wouldn't disappear into a relationship again, wouldn't hand control of herself or her life over to any man ever again, no matter how honorable or wonderful he was.

She was actually glad Denver wasn't coming into work tonight. She needed time to get her bearings, think everything through and make decisions about what she wanted for herself by herself.

The phone rang in her office, and she walked in,

bracing herself in case it was Denver again with more well-meant instructions for how she should live her life. "Hello?"

"Don't you think you should let me in?"

Gina. What the hell was she talking about? "Excuse me?"

"I'd like to come in. But the door is locked."

Oh no. She was *here?* Lindsay walked to her office door and peered through the front door window. There was Gina with her cell phone pressed to her ear.

Oh God.

"What are you doing here?"

"Paying an old friend a visit. What else would I be doing here?"

Lindsay felt like crying. After all the stress she was under from the situation with Denver, Gina picked *now?* "I don't want to talk to you."

"Ouch, honey. That hurts."

"Gina…"

"You know, I can make a lot of noise and attract a lot of attention out here. And when people come to find out what's wrong, I'll have no problem telling them whatever it takes."

Lindsay closed her eyes. Disconnected the call. Walked toward the front door as if she were on her way to her own execution. She didn't have to let Gina in but she wasn't in the mood to deal with the pain in the ass Gina would make of herself standing out on the sidewalk shrieking or whatever else she'd planned. Who knew what she'd tell passers-by. Some manipulative crap or other. That she had a terminal disease and Lindsay was her long-lost sister coldly avoiding a reunion…

She opened the door, wishing it opened out and she could shove it into Gina's face.

"Hi, honey, long time no see." Gina smiled, leaned forward and air-kissed Lindsay's cheek. She hadn't aged a bit in five years. Her hair was still thick and curly, her makeup perfect, her lips full and heavily colored. She still wore clothes that she managed to make look respectable and sexual at the same time. "Aren't you going to invite me in? I'd love to have a look around. I do have a stake in this bar, as you well know. And Denver talks about Chassy all the time."

Lindsay flinched, which was exactly what Gina was trying to get her to do. The barb hit deep. Denver had talked to Gina about Chassy? Was that where she got her information? When exactly was Gina seeing Denver? Lindsay couldn't believe that Denver had spilled anything knowing how it would affect her. He absolutely couldn't be in league with Gina. Nor did she believe he was sleeping with both of them.

At least she refused to torture herself with that possibility. There was hope for her yet.

But why was he talking to her at all? And in what context?

Gina strolled into the bar, glanced around, smiled and stretched out a hand Lindsay just couldn't bring herself to take. "It is so good to see you, Lindsay. You look wonderful."

Lindsay nodded. "What do you want?"

"I was hoping we could sit and talk."

"About what?"

"Old times, new times, future times…"

"You have five minutes."

"I was hoping we could be pleasant about this."

"There isn't anything pleasant about blackmail."

Gina's turn to flinch. She pulled out a chair and sat at a table facing the bar door, shrugged out of her scarlet coat and shook back her curly hair. "While you were thinking over my raise, I wanted to let you know that I've gotten very close to Ralph Gebring. Very close."

Lindsay's stomach clenched. Of course. Not Denver. Ralph. Every time Lindsay had been talking to boring, harmless Ralph, she'd been talking directly to Gina. Undoubtedly everything Gina wanted out of the situation had also been communicated to Ralph. Which meant if Ralph's Aunt Marie invested in the bar, it would be partly because of Gina's influence. That way she could be assured of getting her "raise." It also meant Gina had the power through Ralph to convince his aunt not to invest if Lindsay didn't give in. Lindsay might be able to find private funding somewhere else but she'd have to start from scratch. The process could take weeks, if not months. The Yarn Barn next door went up for sale in March.

Gina had played this brilliantly. She could ask for pretty much anything she wanted right now and knew it. What fun for her to show up and rub her power directly into Lindsay's face. She wouldn't want to miss a minute of Lindsay's agony or her own triumph.

Bitch.

"So what's your point?" Lindsay placed a hand on the back of a nearby chair for support.

"Do I have to spell it out?"

"Gee whiz, Gina, you know better than anyone I have very few brain cells left from all the partying I did." She dropped the sarcasm and the fake smile. "So why don't you spell it out, yes."

"Okay." Gina stretched, catlike and leaned back in her chair. "Here it is. If you want your loan, you need to make sure I get my extra money."

Lindsay had expected every word. Still, it was hard not to react. She forced herself to scan the bottles at the bar, reading label names silently to stay calm. Inside she was reeling. Ralph had a wife and family. He seemed so solid and steady. How could he let such an obvious, conniving witch influence his decisions? Or more to the point, his aunt's? Wouldn't he wonder why the bar seemed so important to Gina?

Gina would stop at nothing to get her way, never had, never would. Lindsay had seen her effect on men before. She could reduce the coldest duty-bound stiff-upper-lip conservative to a mass of unreasoning desire in a matter of hours. And Lindsay was in no position to take major risks.

"Nice deal." She tore her eyes from the bar to Gina's. "How about I think it over and get back to you on—"

"Sorry." Gina's smile shut itself off as if it had a switch. "I need an answer today."

"Call me at midnight, I'll have your answer."

"I'll do better than that. I'll be here." She got up

and pushed in her chair. "I'm meeting Ralph anyway at closing."

"Naturally. Nice touch."

"Lindsay." Gina's eyes softened. She stepped forward and laid her hand against Lindsay's cheek. "You know I hate doing this."

"Right." Lindsay jerked back from Gina's touch and stood straighter, focusing on the solid ground under her feet. "I can see how terribly you're going to suffer making your deposit at the bank."

"I do suffer. I'm not…strong like you are." For a second the carefree hot-mama mask slipped. Lindsay suddenly saw the lines in Gina's forehead and around her eyes, the slight sagging of skin under her chin. "I couldn't do what you've done here. I don't have a shred of work ethic, I know that. I've never been really good at anything but being a parasite."

"And men."

"Yeah. Men." Gina nodded ruefully, flashed a small proud smile. "But I'm getting older and I haven't exactly saved for my retirement."

"So here you are."

She nodded, eyes pleading. "Here I am. I know we can't be friends under the circumstances, but I want you to know…just that…this isn't easy for me."

Lindsay shook her head. She wasn't getting suckered into Gina's bullshit ever again. Even if she was sincere, it didn't change a damn thing about what she was doing. "You want to know what's not easy? Having you show up and—"

Behind Lindsay the bar door opened. Damn. Staff, probably Justin. She had to get Gina out of here fast.

She didn't take her eyes off Gina. "You need to go now."

Gina glanced past Lindsay's shoulder. Her cocky expression dropped off.

Lindsay turned.

Denver. Staring at Gina with recognition but not welcome. "Adele. What are you doing here?"

"Adele?" Lindsay joined Denver in gazing at Gina who for the first time Lindsay could ever remember seemed at a loss.

Of course a few seconds later, she'd recovered beaming at Denver her best sultry invitation. "I didn't think you worked today."

"I don't." He glanced at Lindsay, at Gina, at Lindsay, looking uncomfortable and—was she imagining it?…guilty.

Oh God. She wasn't imagining it. The pain in her heart was agonizing. Something *had* gone on between them. Could this day get any worse?

"Apparently you know each other." There was enough acid in her voice to make Gina beam harder and Denver's Adam's apple take a quick round trip.

"Oh ye-e-es." Gina smiled an intimate artificially whitened smile. "We do."

"Not as well as you're making it seem." Denver's eyes narrowed. He stared at Gina so intently Lindsay expected to see smoking holes appear in her face. Was he figuring it out? He couldn't. He couldn't get involved. Not in this. Not now. "Do you by any chance have another name, *Adele?*"

"Was there something you wanted?" Lindsay spoke curtly to Denver. "We were talking…business here."

Of course Denver picked up right away on her bone-headed hesitation before the word *business,* with a sharp glance in her direction, then another drilling stare at Gina.

Panic took hold in her chest. He'd figured it out.

"I came here to talk to you, Lindsay. Right now, though, I think I'd rather talk to the lovely Gina."

No. No. No.

"I don't know what you'd have to say to her, Denver." She walked in front of him, laid her hand on his chest, her gaze begging him to back off. "We'll only be another minute."

"I'll be less than that. I only have two words for her." He moved Lindsay out of the way, stood tall, hands on his hips, staring down at Gina so grimly, she had the good sense to look discomfited.

"Only two words?" She took refuge in what she did best—oozing sex appeal. "You had a *lot* more to say at the pool."

Denver's flinch felt like a kick to Lindsay's gut. She never, ever wanted to go swimming again.

"Your little party's over, Gina." The furious words were wrenched from his throat. Gina's smile slipped. Even Lindsay got a chill. "Your so-called employment at Chassy is hereby terminated."

"Denver. You can't do this. Don't do this." Lindsay came to life, tugged frantically at his elbow, but she might as well have been trying to bend a lamppost. "You don't understand what's at stake."

"I'd listen to your girlfriend if I were you, Denver, dear. This doesn't concern you." Gina waved him away as if he was a speck of annoying dust. "And that was more than two words."

"You're right. I'll try again. How's this?" He stood back, pointed to the door and pointed her toward it with his other hand. "You're fired."

"Denver, no." Lindsay pushed in front of him, held up both hands to placate Gina whose eyes had narrowed to her catfight worst. "Gina, you can have your raise."

"Oh, it's going to have to be much bigger now." She grabbed her coat off the chair and whipped it over her shoulders. "Much."

"You're not getting another penny."

She ignored Denver, stepped up close to Lindsay. "Ten thousand above what I asked or it's over."

Lindsay's heart pounded. She could barely breathe, barely think. Denver had made everything so much worse. "Ten thousand. I can't—"

"Not another cent, not more, not less. A total of nothing." Denver took Gina's arm and escorted her fairly roughly across the bar to the front entrance. Lindsay rushed to stop him, a hysterical giggle lodged in her throat, aware this must look like some silly slapstick movie, Denver tugging Gina's arm, and Lindsay tugging his.

"Denver. Stop. Think what you're doing."

"I know exactly what I'm doing."

Gina yanked her arm out of his grasp, whirled around and pointed menacingly at his face. "You will regret this!"

"Never. I haven't had this much fun in a long time." Denver opened the door and practically shoved her out into the street. "If you come back to this bar, I'll file a restraining order."

Lindsay stood frozen, watching. This couldn't be happening. Everything ruined. Everything gone. Her business. Her freedom.

"She can kiss her investor goodbye." Gina gestured rudely, shrilly triumphant. "She can look forward to a visit soon from the police."

Denver folded his arms across his chest. "Yeah, I'm shaking in my boots."

Police. Murder charges. Jail time. Everything Lindsay had fought for, everything she'd built could be gone with one phone call. She felt unable to move, unable to act, unable to believe this was really happening. On the one hand she was fascinated and thrilled by Denver's anger and power; on the other beyond horrified at what he was doing and how it could affect her for the rest of her life.

"She has until tonight. Midnight. Then I call the district attorney's office."

"Sorry, which is it? Police or the D.A.? Get your story straight."

Gina sneered. "Both."

"Knock yourself out."

"Fine. Lindsay, congratulations." She drew her coat

tightly around her, her beautiful face distorted with anger. "Once again you've invited in your own ruin. But this time you won't have me to help you clean up."

She stalked off down the sidewalk, her exit marred when she caught her heel in the pavement and her ankle wobbled, throwing her momentarily to one side.

Denver shut the door, braced both hands against it and leaned there. Lindsay didn't move. She didn't think she could. Her body started trembling. Then came anger, rising like a volcano about to erupt.

"What the hell made you think you had the right to do that?"

Denver turned his head, arms still braced against the door, like he was keeping it closed against another onslaught. "Someone had to get this woman off your back."

"Do you realize what you've done?" Her voice was high, her breathing rapid.

"She was bluffing."

"What makes you think that?"

"She wants the money, not trouble. She kept extending her deadline. Tonight at midnight if you haven't called, I guarantee she calls back and says okay, if I don't hear by tomorrow. And then the next day. And then…"

"Easy for you to say. You have nothing at risk here."

Denver took his hands off the door, and turned slowly toward her, his expression neutral but she felt his anger. "No?"

"You aren't the one who would have to go to jail." She flung her arm out accusingly. "You're not the one who needs a loan now or lose any chance of buying the store next door."

"Right. I have absolutely nothing invested in you or in your business. I just decided to piss this woman off on a whim, without thinking of the consequences, without giving you a thought because that's just the kind of macho selfish creep I am."

"You had no right to make business decisions on my behalf."

"That wasn't a business decision. I was protecting you, and your business, from a criminal because you refused to do it. I couldn't stand by and watch your pain any longer."

"You were totally out of line." She was practically panting, tears pushing to escape. She needed every ounce of her willpower to keep them back.

"I'd be totally out of line if I just sat here and let her control you."

"So *you* decided to control me instead."

"Right." He put his hands on his hips and nodded. "Exactly. That's my dream. To control you. That's what this is all about."

"First you move into my house, then into my business." She put her hands to her head, barely aware what she was saying, hating that he could stand there so calmly while she was unravelling. An eerie flashback to her final confrontation with Ty.

"Okay. Maybe you're right. I figured by the time you got around to taking care of us and of Gina, so many pigs would be flying, they'd be taking on passengers."

He took two steps toward her. "I guess I was wrong. I'm taking the job with Alec. I'll find somewhere else to stay. I won't be around to interfere."

"So you ruin my life and then walk out?"

"Lindsay, for God's sake." He held up a hand, controlling himself with obvious effort. "If that's the way you want to look at it, go ahead. Obviously I'm damned whatever I do. You know where you can find me. You know I'd do anything to help you. But I'm sick of having all my efforts and my feelings for you thrown back in my face. You want to handle everything yourself? Be my guest."

In a case of the worst possible timing, Justin came through the front door. "Hey, boss lady. Hey, Denver. What's hap—" he glanced from one to the other, clearly picking up on the tension in the room "—pening?"

"What's happening is that I'm out of here. Effective immediately." He strode to the door, pushed it open, stepped through…and was gone.

13

LINDSAY HUNG UP THE PHONE.

So.

That was that.

The call had been from Ralph Gebring's Aunt Marie. She had given a lot of thought to where she wanted to invest her money, and while she was impressed with Lindsay's ambition and what she had already done with the bar, she had decided instead to invest in an educational program for pregnant teenagers. She'd wished Lindsay well and was sorry she couldn't help.

Lindsay had murmured something as polite as her stunned mind could think of and hung up.

So much for Gina bluffing, on that point at least. Now Lindsay was not only denied her dream of expanding the bar, but she'd have to take seriously Gina's other threats.

Once again Lindsay's talent for making a shambles of her life had caught up with her.

The phone rang again, making her wince. Probably the witch herself, calling to gloat and see if, having absorbed this one delicious blow, Lindsay would change her mind and cough up not only the raise, but the ten thousand extra placation money she demanded after Denver fired her.

Impossible. Lindsay would go bankrupt.

She picked up the receiver, feeling as if all this had to be happening to someone else. "Hello?"

No one.

Which pretty much summed up who Lindsay had to turn to right now. Guess what? She'd made possible exactly what she kept screaming that she wanted. A dream-come-true opportunity to handle everything by herself, to be completely independent.

Congratulations.

Who was she kidding? The bar was empty and cold without Denver and it was too late and too bad for her.

He'd said she knew where to find him if she needed help. But what would she have to offer him? The same thing she'd offered men her whole life. Her misery and her loneliness and her desperation. Denver wasn't like the other men, and she wanted to offer him something better.

All along she'd been asking him to trust that she could handle everything by herself without showing the slightest proof that she actually could. She needed that proof. For him and for herself.

But how? Back to square one, *how* did she get out of this situation?

She stood suddenly, panic and adrenaline spurring her out of her office where she had to slow down to weave through the Friday night crowd toward the bar. She managed to catch Justin's eye as he was shaking a martini, muscles popping out of his clingy black shirt clearly impressing a buxom blond on a stool in front of him.

"Justin, I'm leaving for a few minutes."

He uncapped the shaker and strained the liquid into a frosty glass while the blond looked on appreciatively. "Okay, Lindsay."

She started to turn away, then whipped back. "Did you just call me plain old Lindsay? Not boss woman or whatever else?"

He smiled, reached across the bar and pressed her shoulder gently. "Didn't think you needed any crap from me tonight. Anything you need, you want to take the rest of the night off or whatever, you go ahead. We've got your back."

A lump rose in her throat. She pressed her lips together, nodded brusquely, but let him see in her eyes how much she appreciated the offer even though he didn't know a fraction of what was upsetting her. He probably thought she and Denver had a lover's spat.

She mouthed thank you and managed a smile.

"Go. Go. Get outta here." Justin winked and shooed her away. "You work too hard. Hot babe like you should be playing more, know what I mean?"

She laughed, rolling her eyes, patted the bar sharply twice and made her way through the crowd and out into the blessedly silent, chilly evening. She took several deep breaths of the crisp fresh air, trying to get her pulse to calm down, her brain to clear long enough to think. She did feel slightly more human, though. Justin's words had helped boost her courage.

See, Lindsay? Letting people help was a *good* thing.

She strolled down Beaumont Street, the way she and Denver had strolled the other night except retracing their steps was no fun alone.

She forced her thoughts back where they least wanted to go. If she didn't contact Gina and agree to her demands in the next few hours, Gina had said she would call the police. Denver had thought she was bluffing because if Lindsay went to jail, Gina's income would stop. Her cherished retirement would have to come from other sources.

But he'd also thought she'd been bluffing about Aunt Marie's loan and she hadn't been. Could Lindsay take that risk?

She approached the spot where she and Denver had stood what seemed like months ago, when the snow had been falling in peaceful, fat flakes. That night he'd said he was willing to give her up if he couldn't have all of her. So what had she done? Made sure he couldn't. And good to his word, he'd given her up.

Now she was back at the same spot with what she had asked for. To be left alone. She could very well spend the rest of her life this way.

Either here or behind bars, without Denver, it scarcely made a difference.

Lindsay turned back and strode to the bar. She didn't know what the hell she could do about Gina, but she had to figure something out. She burst into Chassy, avoiding a pair managing to slow dance to one of her and Brooke's favorite Nirvana songs, "Come As You Are," and banged into her office, headed directly for the phone. She'd call Gina and somehow make her see that…that…

"Lindsay."

She whirled around. Brooke walked into her office, followed closely by Joey and Katie.

"We got here just a few minutes ago."

"Justin said you'd gone out briefly."

"So we waited."

Lindsay attempted a smile, but all she could manage was raised eyebrows and what probably looked like a grimace. She didn't want to deal with her half sisters right now. "What's up?"

"We were at Grandpa Henry's house helping get ready for the Valentine's Day party Wednesday."

"Which you still haven't RSVPed that you're coming to."

Lindsay sighed. "Because I'm not really—"

"Of course you are." Joey held out her hands as if no other discussion was necessary. "We can't have the party without you."

Lindsay felt like crying. Too much was coming at her. Too much. She tried to take herself to that cool quiet place, the surface of the moon, but it might as well have had a sign saying "Closed for Repairs." "I don't belong at that party."

The girls exchanged glances. Brooke nodded. "Lindsay, I found something out that I want you to know."

Oh God. What now? Lindsay sank into her desk chair. She couldn't take any more.

"I had lunch with Mom's crazy friend Reba the other day. She said she'd gone to her psychic who did whatever crystal ball thing she does, then told Reba she had to give up the last family secret." Brooke paused, gazing at Lindsay who stared numbly back. Did Brooke expect a reaction? Lindsay had none. Their family, their secrets; she had plenty of her own. "Reba said at first she thought the psychic was talking about Reba's family. Then she realized there was one more thing about Mom's past that she hadn't told us."

Lindsay groaned. "What, I'm not really Daisy's daughter?"

Katie looked at her incredulously. "Why would you say that?"

"That's what kind of day it's been."

"Uh-oh." Joey pounced on her statement, frowning. "We want to hear about that. Brooke, go on, tell her."

"Reba told me that when Mom was twenty-one, she'd fallen for a 'complete cad,' as Reba called him, who got Mom pregnant with you. His name was Nathan Sprecht."

Lindsay sat motionless. Her father. A complete cad, how fitting. Obviously Lindsay had spent most of her life seeking out men just like Daddy without even realizing it.

What a touching tribute.

"We knew that. What we didn't know…" Brooke's eyes filled. She looked down at her folded hands. "Was that he came back two years later, swearing he had reformed and would marry her—and he got Mom pregnant again."

"Then the jerk disappeared. Again." Katie rolled her eyes, but they were shining, and her mouth was curved in a smile.

"So you and Brooke…" Joey gestured between the two of them, obviously impatient for Lindsay to catch on.

Brooke grinned, a tear spilling over onto her smooth perfect cheek. "We're full sisters, Lindsay. We have the same mother and father."

Lindsay gaped at her, too stunned to speak. Full sisters. She and Brooke. She mentally tallied up their height, widow's peak, long slender fingers, even a mutual passion for Nirvana.

A whole sister. Not half.

Tears started streaming down her face. She sobbed soundlessly, and was enveloped in three pairs of arms all at once.

At the same moment, everyone's sobs started mixing with giggles.

"Honestly." Brooke wiped her eyes. "I'm a mess."

"Hallmark moment." Katie dabbed at her cheek with a tissue. "I'm a mess too."

"Me three," Joey said thickly. "Enough of this. We need to kidnap Lindsay, go out and celebrate. She can tell us about her crappy day somewhere we can all cut loose."

"Karaoke!" Katie crowed. "We found this fabulous place we want you to see, Lindsay. It would be perfect to take Tanya to next month for her Martini Dare since we stole hers last month and she got her lab partner all by herself."

"I can't."

"Aw, c'mon." The three women chimed at once.

Lindsay shook her head. Met each of their eyes in turn, lingering on Brooke's. She wasn't alone. She had a family.

And if she could pull this off, she'd have another chance to be with Denver. He'd been willing to give her up if he couldn't have all of her. Now she was willing to risk everything to have all of him.

She took a deep breath. "I'm in trouble. I need your help. I can't do this by myself."

Ironically, it had been tremendously easy. Three sentences, about a dozen words, one obvious concept. *I. Need. Help.*

Immediately their three faces radiated concern.

"Of course."

"Anything."

"What is it?"

"You better sit down." Busting with sudden adrenaline—but without panic this time—Lindsay pushed her chair over to Katie and perched on the desk while Brooke and Joey found a chair and table and sat down.

Lindsay faced them, her one full sister, and two half sisters…no. Her sisters. Period. Three of them, waiting, poised and calm even in their obvious anxiety on her behalf. She had the feeling that if she told them they needed to jump off a mountain for her, they'd charter a plane, get there and jump before she even had the chance to explain why.

And she hadn't even been generous enough to tell them she'd go to their party. Someone better be baking humble pie nearby because she was due a healthy helping.

Another deep breath and she told them everything. Started hesitantly, then picked up speed until she was rushing in her haste to be open with these women, until everything she'd told Denver was now told to her family.

Her family. Only one person in this world was more important to her than these three women. If he'd meet her halfway in this battle, the battle would be over with all sides victorious.

"My God, Lindsay!" Joey had her hands plastered to her temples. "Why the hell didn't you tell us sooner? I'm a lawyer for heaven's sakes. I have connections all over the place. And Grandpa Henry knows the Suffolk County D.A., he's the son of an old military buddy. Plus Sebastian's best friend is a cop. We can fix this for you in a day."

Lindsay looked at her watch. "I've got two and a half hours."

STAY AWAY. DENVER HURLED A STACK of books into a box. *Just stay away.* He tucked the books neatly against the box's edge and dumped in another stack. Then, as he'd done roughly every twenty seconds, he checked his watch. Eleven-fifteen. Chassy would be nearing last call, and closing in forty-five minutes. Gina's deadline. Midnight.

Every instinct in his body told him to drop the books, forget the stupid packing, get into his car and drive as fast as he could to Chassy to make sure Lindsay stayed out of harm's way.

Then what? Lindsay accused him of trying to take over, of controlling her and yeah, okay, he could see her point. Maybe he'd gone from total noninterference into overdrive without giving her a chance to adjust. Hell, desperate times called for desperate measures, and the thought of that…woman—he used the term loosely— Gina, funneling off cash that Lindsay had nearly exhausted herself to make honestly—well, it didn't make him warm and fuzzy. So he hadn't acted that way.

That Gina as Adele had followed him to the pool, that she'd been at all attractive to him, that she'd touched him, that he'd even mentioned Lindsay and Chassy to her, let alone told her some of what was going on there, made him feel sick, which had made him even angrier. Thank God she mentioned Ralph Gebring's role in informing on Lindsay's situation, because if Denver had thought Lindsay's troubles were caused even partly by him, however inadvertently, Gina probably could have filed assault charges.

He crumpled newspaper fiercely, stuffing it in the cracks between the rows of books. He'd be moving into Jack's place tomorrow into the tiny guest bedroom. Denver would be spending most of his time at the clinic starting Monday anyway. He needed little more than access to a bathroom and a bed. A far cry from what he'd envisioned living with Lindsay.

Another glance at his watch. Eleven-twenty. Damn it. *Stay away, Denver. She doesn't want you there. She insists she doesn't need you there.* He could end up making everything worse, barging in and forcing Gina's hand. He'd done that already once today. How could he live with himself, though, if Gina did call the police? Why hadn't he spent his time wisely, making phone calls to find people who could really help her? Instead he'd turned to macho strong-arm tactics that had little chance of success. He wasn't a lawyer, he had no idea what kind of chance Lindsay had of being charged with murder, let alone surviving a trial. He couldn't believe anyone could listen to her and not believe everything she said but he'd never want to put that to the test. What if he was wrong? What if she got twelve Ginas on the jury?

He sealed the box, stacked it on top of two other boxes by the window, marked it, Books.

Eleven twenty-three.

He tossed the marker onto his bed, stood there, hands on his hips, brooding. Brooding some more.

To hell with it. There was no way he was going to be able to leave Lindsay alone to face that horror show. Even if Lindsay threw him back out onto the street, at least she'd know he was there if she needed him. Even if she didn't. Call him Mr. Masochist, he couldn't leave this woman alone, whatever the cost to his heart and sanity.

He launched himself down the stairs, relieved as hell finally to be acting, grabbed his jacket on the way out the door and started up his car. Twenty minutes later he was parked, having miraculously driven up when someone was just pulling out of a space half a block from Chassy and across the street. From there he could keep an eye on anyone who went in or came out. When the last of the staff left, he could at least peek. Since he still had his key he could go in if intervention was necessary.

Five minutes later, a group of three left the bar, staggering slightly, kids out on a bender. Last ones? Yes. He saw a shadow through the door window—Lindsay, locking up. Ten minutes later, Justin and three waitresses left.

She was alone. And it was midnight.

He waited until Justin and his gaggle of gigglers had disappeared into the darkness, then got out of his car and walked quietly toward Chassy, quelling a sudden ludicrous image of himself as Gary Cooper in *High Noon*, walking the empty main street in preparation for a gun battle he was sure to lose.

As he reached the door and was peering inside, he heard a light step behind him and turned.

Gina.

"Hello, Denver." She smiled distractedly and he resisted the urge to punch her in the nose. "You 'n Lindsay patch things up?"

"Last time I checked that was none of your business."

"Aww, c'mon." She pouted and patted his chest, however without the degree of cocky triumph he expected. She didn't look quite like herself—had she been crying? "Have you come to watch the fun?"

"What fun would that be, Gina?"

She smiled tightly and rapped on the door. "Payday."

His gut tightened. Lindsay had caved. To save her

business. To save herself. He couldn't stand it. Why hadn't she let anyone help? "I can't wait. Is Ralph waiting for you? You're in on this together?"

"Ralph can' be here." Her words stumbled into each other. She hadn't been crying. She'd been drinking.

"What a shame."

"His *wife* needs him." Her narrow-eyed sneer was ruined when she took an involuntary step backward and her lids flew wide in alarm.

Not drinking. Drunk.

"Oh, wow, needing her own husband, how inconsiderate of her."

Her icy stare meant his sarcasm had penetrated. He found this deeply satisfying.

Lindsay's shape came to the window; Denver's heart beat painfully. She opened the door, saw him and did a double take. Her features lifted instantly into joy, then just as quickly fell into dismay. "Denver. What are you doing here?"

I came to help. The phrase would be ludicrous. She might need his help but she didn't want it and had told him so repeatedly. He should have stayed home. But what kind of man would he be to leave her in such a mess?

"I couldn't stay away." He held her eyes, saw hers soften, and his heart leapt.

"This is all tremendously touching, but it's freezing out here, and I have somewhere to be, so can we get on with it?"

"Of course." Lindsay stepped away, opening the door

wider, watching Gina curiously as she passed. Lindsay noticed too. And for reasons he couldn't understand, looked suddenly pleased. Maybe she knew something about Gina drunk that she could use to her advantage?

God, he hoped so. Right now it didn't seem Lindsay had any advantage at all. He suspected Gina had been celebrating that fact most of the evening before she showed up.

He filed in behind Gina, keeping his eye on Lindsay. The momentary pleasure on her face had gone. She was controlled as usual, but he sensed her tension. He wanted to sweep her up in his arms and carry her off to a tropical paradise where he could feed her grapes and pamper her around the clock. Not to mention ravish her hourly. Would she ever let him?

Lindsay drew out a chair at the only table in the room with the chairs still on the floor. "Have a seat and we'll talk."

Denver approached, but took a chair off a table several yards away, turning the seat backwards. He sat and folded his arms along its back. He wanted to make it clear he was here only as an observer, Lindsay's hired thug. That the business at hand was between the two ladies—or rather one lady and one utter bitch.

Lindsay glanced over at him in surprise, then gave the tiniest hint of a smile. Approval? Maybe she'd understood his intended statement.

Gina pulled up her chair and folded her hands on the table, leaning forward so her lush artificial cleavage plumped up from her low-cut top like fleshy water balloons. Had he really been tempted? It seemed impossible. "So we're in agreement?"

"How about a drink?" Lindsay was already on her way to the bar, returned with a glass of ice, a bottle of Bombay Sapphire and a dish of lime wedges. "On the house."

"You remembered my favorite." Gina's eyes softened, like a mother's at the unexpected sight of her baby.

"Sure." Lindsay squeezed the lime over the ice, ran the fruit around the rim and added a generous amount of gin. "Bottoms up."

"You're not joining me?"

"My big drinking days are over, Gina."

"Pity. You used to be a lot of fun." Gina lifted the glass in a toast. "Here's to old times."

Lindsay's expression froze on her face. Denver was pretty sure if she'd had a glass in front of her, she would more likely have tossed the contents in Gina's face than joined in the toast. "So. You want ten thousand more than what I was already paying you for your silence."

Denver inhaled sharply. Immediately Lindsay sent him an urgent warning look. Damn it, she expected him to sit here and watch her throw away everything she'd worked for?

"If I don't pay, you go to the police—"

"Lindsay." Her name burst out of him. He couldn't stand this.

Another look from her, this one murderous. He bowed his head, instructing himself to relax. Something told him this moment was really the end. If he interfered now his chances of a life with Lindsay would be gone forever. She'd make sure of that. He'd read it in her eyes.

But if he sat back and let her hand her life over rather than accept help, he couldn't stay. He couldn't be with someone who didn't fight for what she wanted, who kept him so determinedly on the outside.

Okay. So be it. This was her show.

He met her gaze and nodded, feeling as if an elephant had just stomped on his heart. She'd won. He'd stay out of it. When this little sick joke of a meeting was over, he'd leave Chassy and he wouldn't come back.

Lindsay rewarded him with a brief smile that hurt more than the elephant. A hell of a lot more.

"If I don't pay you, you'll go to the police and eventually testify in court that I pushed Ty down the stairs with intent to kill…" Her voice dropped and got husky. "And you'll swear his last words to me were tender words of love rather than what they really were."

She looked helplessly at Gina, eyes pleading. Denver followed her gaze. He hated looking at Gina, but he couldn't bear to see Lindsay's defeat.

Gina swallowed her gin, the ice rushing suddenly from the bottom of the glass to fall around her mouth. She put the drink back on the table, hand shaking slightly, then stared down at it, fingers drumming along its side. "He was quite the bastard to me too, you know."

"Ty?" Lindsay's voice grew immediately gentle.

"Yeah." She gave a bitter laugh. "Quite the bastard. You didn't know."

"You mean…he hit you too?" Lindsay sounded

amazed. Denver looked at her curiously. Ty was clearly a giant jerk. Why would that surprise her?

"I think he got off on it." Gina hunched her shoulders, then dropped them. "I had a dream once that I killed him and woke up wanting to make it come true."

"I didn't realize you and he…"

"I know. I know you didn't." Gina exhaled suddenly, a breath that sounded nearly like a sob. "When Ty went bad, God, he could top them all. Vicious bastard."

"The worst." Lindsay spoke soothingly, sympathetically, in a low, coaxing tone. "At the end, right before I lost it, when he said he loved me and would keep me with him forever…"

"Yeah. Sick, sick bastard. Controlling. Abusive."

"You knew what he really meant." Lindsay poured Gina more gin.

"Oh yeah. I knew. When he took a woman, he wouldn't let go." Gina picked up the glass and shook her head. "He wouldn't. He'd have killed you, me, anyone rather than let us go."

"Those words." Lindsay spoke soothingly. "When he said them to me it was like, I don't know…"

"He was goading you and you snapped. Anyone would have. I would have pushed him too." She sighed again, suppressed a belch. "Men. Can't live with 'em—"

"Can't push 'em down the stairs." Lindsay chuckled, looking nothing like a woman about to lose her business. Denver's hope rose from the pit of despair it had sunk into while listening to the horrible replay of Ty's death. Lindsay was up to something.

"You're okay, Lindser. Sucks we had to meet like this again. But…" Gina pushed her glass to one side and slapped her palms on the table. "That's all ancient history. I want my money. Here and now."

Lindsay smiled. A triumphant smile. "Here and now, Gina."

The door to her office opened. People started coming out, reminding Denver somewhat absurdly of clowns spilling out of a tiny car at the circus. Brooke. Joey. Katie. Joey's boyfriend Sebastian holding an official looking briefcase. A uniformed cop…

Denver's heart started pounding. He glanced at Gina, saw the shock on her face, the color draining out of it and he laughed, he couldn't help it. If this hadn't been a serious proceeding, with the cop striding forward to arrest Gina on a charge of blackmail, he would have picked Lindsay up, dragged her into her office and kissed her for the rest of her life.

14

LINDSAY ENTERED HER APARTMENT, took off her coat and tossed it wearily toward the hook where she usually hung it. It missed and slid forlornly to the floor. She couldn't be bothered to pick it up. She'd been tired before, plenty of times, but this felt like an entirely new world of exhaustion.

And yet…she'd done it. She was free—or nearly. A formality Joey had said, once the D.A. reviewed the details. Admittedly, the realization hadn't sunk in yet. She'd spent so much of her life under a dark cloud that now that the sun was about to come out, she felt apprehension along with the joy.

The police had taken her down to the station with Gina for questioning. She'd told the story of Ty's death, not sparing herself this time, every detail as she remembered it, not what Gina had coached her to say. Then she'd launched into the story of the blackmail as she'd told it to Denver and to her sisters. Only this time she had hope, instead of self-loathing. Gina's crime was on record. The details of Ty's death were on record. Joey had assured her that, in light of the time that had passed, the obvious good character Lindsay had shown since the accident and Gina's additional evidence of Ty's abuse, the D.A. wouldn't reopen the case and press charges.

Lindsay was pretty sure factoring in the influence of Henry Winfield wouldn't hurt, though her sisters had avoided mentioning that again.

She could hardly believe only a few hours earlier she was finally confiding in her siblings. Her adoptive parents had been right. It took more than blood to make a family. Discovering her half sisters last fall had been earth-shaking. Likewise the revelation that she and Brooke shared two parents. However, her sisters' determination to help her at all costs had meant the most. The way Brooke, Joey and Katie had come through for her was like nothing she'd ever experienced. Gina's attempt at picking up the pieces of Lindsay's life after Ty's death had been utterly self-serving. Scott and Laura Downing's sale of Chassy had been generous, but they had benefited too. Her sisters had no motive to help Lindsay…other than their love for her.

And Denver had no motive to show up again tonight after she'd sent him away so rudely, except…the same? Now that her life seemed to be coming back together, she even dared hope where he was concerned. More than hope. Longing, and love of her own. She'd asked her sisters for help. She'd beaten back the threat of Gina. She'd defused her past by exposing it and by finally making peace with the law. For the first time Lindsay had much more to offer a man than need and insecurity and fear.

Drained as she was, a smile was on her lips when she stepped into her kitchen and saw her message light blinking. Her heart sped up. Denver hadn't come to the police station earlier. He'd mumbled something about needing to pack, given her a quick hug of congratulations, saying that he'd see her later. She hoped when the dust from this extraordinary day settled, that he'd understand and give her one more chance. After giving her so many other chances, all of which she'd blown…

She hoped he wasn't upset she hadn't turned to him. Joey had been on the phone to Sebastian seconds after hearing Lindsay's story of Ty's death and Gina's blackmail. Then Brooke had tackled Grandpa Henry—or rather had managed to extract the D.A.'s phone number from the housekeeper Louise. Within half an hour Sebastian and his cop friend Hunter McAllister had arrived, heard Lindsay's story and helped plan the battle strategy.

It had all happened so quickly and easily. Lindsay couldn't bear thinking of all the months she'd spent closed off like a crab in a trap, claws up, unable to see that if she just turned around, the exit was right there. She'd been so full of guilt, so possessed by the victim mentality that had kept her in abusive relationships, so convinced that she was in the wrong, so afraid of being punished for Ty's accident and losing everything she held dear, that she'd been blind to the simple fact that what Gina was doing was also illegal and punishable.

And speaking of traps, Gina had walked into the trap Lindsay set, so smoothly and completely, she still couldn't believe it. Right out of Gina's pouty mouth, a confession not only to blackmail, but that she was planning false testimony against Lindsay in court, in front of a doctor, a lawyer, a policeman and three Winfields. You couldn't get more reputable witnesses on your side than that.

The only surprise had been Denver showing up when she'd been so sure he'd washed his hands of her stubborn inability to let him in. She'd nearly melted at the sight of him at her door, her knight in shining armor, though his presence during the interview with Gina had both bolstered and unnerved her. Of course he'd thought she was caving in to Gina's demands. Of course he'd been outraged and tried to stop her. It had nearly killed Lindsay to stomp on what he was offering once again, even knowing what was at stake, even knowing it was the last time she ever would. He must understand now why she couldn't have let him interfere.

And yet, even thinking she was ruining her life, he had respected her and backed off without asking why, simply because she made it clear she wanted him to. She saw the effort pulling away had cost him and loved him all the more. After that her need for boundaries against him had vanished. A bizarre paradox—as long as he respected those she set, she no longer felt she needed any.

Lindsay pressed Play on the answering machine, desperately praying for Denver's voice—and then realizing with a wry laugh that it made no difference if he called or not because she was going to call him. Goodbye Lindsay the crab and Lindsay the victim. She'd go to him, unencumbered by her past, and offer all of herself this time. All of herself and all of her future.

Three messages, one from each sister, thrilled for her victory, ecstatic over her release from her torment.

She was one of them.

First thing in the morning she'd RSVP to Grandpa Henry that yes, she'd very much like to come to the Winfield Valentine's Day ball.

First she wanted to make sure she'd have a date.

DENVER TURNED OVER, THUMPED his pillow into shape for the fortieth time and sighed. He couldn't sleep. Which he supposed was understandable, given that it wasn't every night he tried to rescue the would-be love of his life from a blackmailer only to discover she had the entire situation under control with witnesses and police at the ready. It hadn't been easy to pull back when she asked him to, but it had been a revelation. He already knew, boy how he already knew, that she could take care of herself—but now he knew she could take care of herself by allowing people to help her too. Maybe even by asking them to.

Just not him.

He sat up in total frustration, then threw off the covers and officially gave up the doomed effort to sleep. He'd backed off and let Lindsay handle the blackmail situation. He'd backed off and not insisted on accompanying her to the police station. He'd backed off by not calling to make sure she was okay now though every part of him wanted to.

His only fear was that if he kept backing off further and further eventually he'd lose sight of her.

He stood and stretched, taking in the dim shapes of stacked boxes around him. Three o'clock. He'd go for a swim. Might as well see if he could work off this sleep-interfering manic energy with some laps.

He dug around briefly in a suitcase for his bathing suit, then gave up. Why bother? No one would be there tonight. Gina was resting uncomfortably c/o the U.S. Government. The Robinsons were due back the next day on the same flight as his parents. He did toss his jacket over his pajamas and stuff his feet into boots he'd left by the door since he wasn't a big fan of frost-bite.

Outside the air was crisp and dry, the half moon cut a sharp, thick letter *C* into the blackness overhead. A car door slammed behind him on the street—another night owl, likely coming home from a situation much less complicated than his had been.

He unlocked the sliding door to the pool area, went in, breathing the moist, chlorinated air. He jacked up the thermostat as the Robinsons insisted he do when he was using the pool, leaving off the lights as usual to swim in near darkness.

After taking off his parka, kicking off the boots, sliding out of his pajamas, he dived in without testing the water. Chilly, but not unbearable. He swam a few laps, then a few more, the physical exercise relaxing him, the water's touch soothing his heated skin.

He retrieved the Robinsons' giant yellow raft,

dragged it into the water and clambered on, hands clasped under his head, watching the moon shining through the glass ceiling.

So now what? Tomorrow he moved in with Jack. Monday he started his new job, new life. And Lindsay? Now that her demons were vanquished, would she want to be with him or not?

How much more could he struggle to reach out to her? Tonight had been a change, but how much of one? Enough to make what he wanted also what she wanted?

Too many questions, no answers.

A noise made him turn suddenly, his brain registering in an instant that he hadn't locked the door behind him. Not *Adele* this time, it couldn't be.

A tall figure. Female. Long hair. Wearing a parka, and…wait, not a parka, she was taking that off.

Wearing pants, and a shirt that—

His heart beat faster. A grin spread over his face. He slid into the water and swam to the shallow end. No, wait, no pants. Those were off too, beside her parka.

A shirt, then, a long-sleeved black turtleneck that—

Mmm. His cock stirred, even in the chilly water.

No turtleneck.

"Come on in. The water's fine."

"Hi, Denver." She spoke softly, sounded tired. He couldn't imagine how exhausted she must be after today, after the past several days, weeks, months. And yet…she was here. She'd chosen to be with him.

"You know my name—didn't catch yours."

"Ha ha."

"Lindsay…" He found himself emotional even saying her name. "Are you okay?"

Her laughter floated to him over the undulating water, gladdening his heart. Lindsay didn't laugh enough. "How many times do you think you've asked me that over the last year, Denver?"

"Hundreds."

"What have I always said?"

"That you're fine."

"Ask me again."

He smiled. Everything about this visit felt positive and good and right. "Are you okay, Lindsay?"

"I'm tired. Really tired. And sad for what I had to do tonight. I'm also proud that I did it and grateful to the friends that helped me. And right now…"

"Yes?" His voice had dropped. He could barely produce tone.

"Right now I need to tell you that I love you. And I wanted to be with you so badly tonight that I took a chance and drove over. And there you were coming out of your house, and over here."

This time he couldn't speak. He tried, but his voice jammed in his throat behind the huge ball of emotion blocking it. *She loved him.* Those words had actually come out of her mouth. Freely. He was stunned. Joyous. Overwhelmed. All of the above.

"So I decided it was time I came swimming with you. And spent the night. And took tomorrow away from the bar to help you move."

"Move?" He stared, knowing he probably looked

and sounded like a complete idiot. She was going to take a day off. For him.

"Yes, move. Load belongings in vehicle at old address, unload at new one…" She lifted her hands toward him. "If you want."

"I want." Miraculously his voice came out, croaky and emotional, but it worked. "I want it all. Yes to everything."

"Good." She'd taken off her shoes and walked toward him in a dark underwear set with lighter-colored flowers on it that made her look sexy as hell and somehow sweet at the same time. She reached the edge of the pool, a few feet down from where he stood, put a toe in and grimaced. "Brrrr. What are you, a polar bear?"

He grinned. "A fierce one. A hungry one."

"Oooh." Life had come back into her voice, and now playfulness. "I better be careful."

"Uh-huh. And, I was thinking…" He swam over until he was at her feet. "You should take your underwear off before you come in. You know, to keep it dry."

"Ahhh, I see your point. That is a good idea." Her voice turned low and husky. "Would you like to watch?"

Any strides he'd made in getting his vocal cords to function properly were immediately erased along with most of his brain as the blood rushed south. He managed to get out a syllable that sounded like, "Yunh."

She stepped back until her tall, slim body was silhouetted against the light wall of the pool room. Listening to some internal rhythm, she began to sway, unselfconsciously, his fantasy come true in lingerie that was hot as a wet dream and demure as a bride all at the same time. Her hands drifted up her stomach and rested over her breasts. She arched and caressed herself.

He imagined the softness of the fabric under his own fingers, the firm weight of her breasts, feeling it was entirely likely he'd pass out and drown.

Her hands met in the center of her chest, the material tensed and gave way, slid over her shoulders, down her arms, dropping onto the tile. She was topless, nipples dark, then hidden from sight again under her loving touch. Her hips undulated, their symmetry enhanced by the strip of black lace, making a low, wide triangle he wanted to bury his face into.

As he stared, her hands invaded his focus, fingers disappearing under the material, meeting over her sex, then parting and moving to the side, then back over her buttocks as she gyrated to one side to give him visual access. She stroked her gorgeous ass, arching her back, rotating her hips, making him crazy with desire. Then slowly she edged the panties down, flipped her long hair around to watch him watching her and stepped out of the black lace. She smiled mischievously…then tossed the panties over her shoulder.

Naked. Creamy skin, dark nipples, darker triangle of hair at her thighs, and in her fingers a small black square which he realized was a condom and loved her even more for careful planning.

No longer able to bear not touching her, he hoisted himself out of the water, strode toward her and lifted her in his arms.

"You're wet!" She locked her arms around his neck, pretending outrage.

"Not as wet as you're going to be."

"Mmm." Moving forward for a kiss, she was completely surprised when he dumped her into the pool and jumped back in, chuckling at her squeal of outrage.

"It's cold!"

"So?" He lunged for her, hauled her up against him and kissed her, once, twice, three times, he was starving, heart hammering to get out of his chest. "We'll heat it up."

"Denver…" She was laughing, splashed him. He couldn't stop smiling, splashed her back and got drenched again.

Lindsay was having fun.

"Here. Climb on here." He swam over, retrieved the raft and held it steady for her.

"It won't tip?" She eyed it dubiously.

"It might. So?"

"I don't know…"

"C'mon, live on the wild side."

She laughed. Again! And climbed on rather clumsily. The sight of her naked ass sprawled across the edge just about sent him over his own edge.

He joined her, nearly tipping the raft over, and they both laughed, desperately trying to stay on.

Then they were on together, balanced. Silence fell as the emotion grew, the water smoothed itself around them. "Lindsay."

He reached for her, kissed her over and over, tasting cool chlorine and warm skin, touching, stroking her. The raft bobbed gently, made a leisurely circle around the pool.

He put the condom on, moved carefully over her as she shifted center. Miraculously the raft held steady. Miraculously it didn't tip when he entered her, when he whispered her name, when they moved together, stars overhead, water underneath, the two of them, face-to-face, rocking on their own private island.

When she came, she said his name. When he did, he whispered hers. Never had he felt so connected to another person. Never had he been so sure she was the one or so triumphant and happy that he sensed no fear in her this time, no resistance. She gave herself completely; he did the same.

Afterward, they lay slowly drifting across the water, lazily dipping a hand in now and then, the water trickling off their fingers onto each other's skin.

"Denver?"

"Mmm?" He could barely make himself speak through the heavy sleepy contentment.

"I had a nightmare about being in this pool with dark shadows under me that I thought were going to attack." She gave a contented sigh. "Now I'm here with you, they're not there anymore."

"No. Gone." He squeezed her closer. "All of them."

"And Denver?"

"Mmm." He could listen to her say his name for hours at a time.

"I also want to say that I'm so sorry I gave you such a hard—"

"—On?" He touched her cheek. "Don't apologize anymore, Lindsay. You were up against an impossible situation, and you handled it the way your instincts and experience told you to handle it. I'm just glad you trusted your sisters to help you out. They're good allies to have in this town. In any town."

"They're an awesome force." She draped her arm over his chest, rested her head on his shoulder. She fit him perfectly. Forever.

"So you're going to help me move tomorrow?"

"Yes." She lifted her head and watched him. "Into my place. If you still want to."

Adrenaline hit. He turned his head and grinned at her. "Uh, yes, I want to, Lindsay. You have no idea how much I want to."

"And I have a favor to ask."

He let his features fall, feigning annoyance. "What now?"

She giggled. "Wednesday night is the Winfields' annual Valentine's Day ball with everyone who's anyone in Boston invited. The girls want me there and I owe it to them to go. It will be in their mansion, and I'll be horribly intimidated and would really like your company as my date."

"So wait, wait." He held up a hand, sure that happiness could not get any more intense than this. "Let me get this straight. What you're actually saying…is that you need my *help?*"

"Don't push it."

"That you can't go to this party unless I'm with you?

That without me you'd be lost, unable to cope, completely adrift and—"

The rest of his sentence was completed underwater. He came up sputtering and immediately bumped up the raft so she went under too. When she came up he was there, arms around her, kissing her again. Would he ever get enough?

"You might not have heard this but I can take care of myself." She pushed her hair out of her face, looking at him coyly. "I'd just love it if now and then you wanted to take care of me too. And vice versa."

"It's a deal." He rested his forehead against hers, his heart painful with emotion. "I love you, Lindsay. I always will."

Her smile lit up the pool better than any light could. "Those are pretty big words, cowboy."

"I mean them."

She nodded, sobering. "I feel that way too."

"Your favorite mount?"

"Yes, Denver." She laughed, put her arms around his shoulders, wrapped her legs around his waist, tipped her head back and laughed again, deep and joyous and free. "My wildest ride ever."

Epilogue

"READY?" DENVER REACHED ACROSS the car to squeeze Lindsay's hand, which was icy, she knew. They had just pulled up in Denver's Camry to Henry and Evelyn Winfield's imposing brick colonial mansion. Immediately the car doors were opened by uniformed help. A white-gloved hand was extended to help her out into the freakishly warm temperatures for February, hovering near fifty degrees.

Any calm that Lindsay had managed to save up disappeared under this formal onslaught.

"I'm ready." What else could she say? She couldn't cower in the car for the rest of the party, though come to think of it, she'd like to.

Denver squeezed her hand again and got out, leaving the keys in the ignition for the valet. Lindsay took the valet's gloved hand, afraid it would be rude not to and managed to exit the car without tripping. It had been a lot of years since she'd worn heels this high.

Having made it out of the car, she smoothed the folds of her gown. She'd bought it with Brooke, Joey and Katie on another afternoon shopping trip. The price nearly choked her, but she managed to pretend she dropped that many hundreds of dollars on outfits all the time. The look on Denver's face when he saw her in the dress tonight made it worth every penny. In fact, they were nearly late to the party. Ahem.

The gown was many times more elegant than anything she'd ever worn. Its full ankle-length skirt of sheer black material wafted over a gray satin sheath. The tight strapless bodice glittered with silver beads that also sparkled in jagged stripes bolting down the skirt. Brooke's earrings dangled from Lindsay's lobes, cascades of sparkling stones Lindsay was too nervous to ask whether they were real diamonds or not. Brooke had found the dress at Neiman Marcus and insisted it would be perfect for the event. Of course Lindsay had no choice but to trust her.

Denver came up beside her, put his hand at the small of her back, grinned down at her, still a couple of inches taller, even with her in heels. In his tuxedo he looked about as handsome as any man she'd ever seen, as if he was born to formal wear, which he probably was. He glanced around at the extensive grounds and what would be gorgeous formal gardens in season; the luxury cars lined up on the driveway and in the estate parking lot; and the sparkling women and expensively outfitted men emerging from them.

"Nothing intimidating about this crowd, huh?"

Lindsay's smile stuttered onto her face. "Yeah. I've seen most of them at the bar sucking down Budweisers."

"I knew they looked familiar." He grinned and

offered his arm. "Madam Beckham, may I escort you into these hallowed halls?"

"As long as we can go to some neighborhood dive afterward to remind ourselves reality still exists."

He gave her the loving look that made her insides gooey and sweet. "I'm with you."

They walked up the front steps toward the ivied brick mansion's entranceway, and even more intimating, the regal elderly couple at the door greeting the guests.

"The admiral," Lindsay whispered, trying not to sound awed. He was exactly as she pictured him—except he wore a tux instead of full uniform—about a million years old, but with a still-commanding presence, a hook nose he could look down and piercing blue eyes under bushy brows that could sum you up and dismiss you in a heartbeat. Beside him, his wife Evelyn, not a white hair out of place, in a cream gown with matching embroidered jacket that fitted as if it were made for her, which it undoubtedly had been. Pearls and tiny diamonds cascaded at her throat and dripped off her ears. Even her wrinkles were flattering.

Lindsay really, really didn't want to meet them. Nothing in her past had prepared her for what to say or how to act around these people, except reading novels and watching period movies. This was real aristocracy, as close as anyone got to it in this country.

The line moved forward. They climbed another step. Evelyn and Henry greeted each guest warmly by name and asked each one a question about his or her family or home or business. Charming, gracious, tremendously well-bred. And part of Lindsay's new family.

She wanted to laugh. When people had come to her parents' house for dinner, there was a bag of chips on the coffee table, vodka in the freezer and her father would yell, "Come in, it's open!" from where he sat on the couch watching TV.

Whadya know, Lindsay's first ever twinge of nostalgia.

The next guest presented a perfectly wrapped present and Lindsay's blood ran even colder.

"I didn't bring a gift. It's an anniversary party," she whispered to Denver.

He smiled into her eyes. "You did bring one."

"Oh thank God, you got them something?" Her relief was immense. She owed him big time.

"You brought them something rare and precious they've never had before." He kissed her temple. "You."

Lindsay rolled her eyes, knowing he could see how pleased she was by his compliment. The next couple in line had no gift. Maybe they'd be okay.

Then, gulp, it was their turn.

"Good evening." Evelyn held out her hand to Lindsay, smile in place, eyes looking blankly between her and Denver. "Welcome to our home."

"I'm Lindsay. Beckham." She sounded like a little girl responding to a teacher on her first day of school. "I'm your— Daisy was my—"

"Lindsay." Evelyn's hand tightened. Her gaze focused on Lindsay's face. "My goodness, the resemblance to Brooke is striking. I can't think how I missed it. Welcome, my dear. Henry, this is Lindsay."

The admiral nodded, examining her no doubt for flaws.

"Happy Anniversary to you both." She felt like Eliza Doolittle on show at the prince's ball, hoping to conceal traces of her lowly origins, except Evelyn and Henry knew the bare minimum of hers. "This is Denver Langston."

Denver and Evelyn exchanged all the right pleasantries which meant Lindsay was thrust opposite the formidable Admirable Henry Winfield.

The back of her head was starting to ache. She loosened her smile. "You have a lovely home."

"Lindsay." He took her hand in his bony one. The strength of his grip was a total surprise, and yet it probably shouldn't have been. "Welcome to the family. My granddaughters are very fond of you."

"They're wonderful. They've done so much for me." She hesitated, not sure if she was allowed to bring up the decidedly non-Winfield situation he'd helped bail her out of. But since it was unlikely she'd see a whole lot of him in the future, and she was extremely grateful… "Thank you, Admiral Winfield, for interceding on my behalf with—"

"That was nothing." He patted her hand, still held in his noble grip. "Nothing I wouldn't do for any of my granddaughters. And I think you better call me Henry like the rest of them or I'll get confused."

She swallowed. He considered her his granddaughter? "Thank you."

"Enjoy the party. We'll expect you at all the family dinners from now on, young lady."

"Yes, sir." She smiled at his look of censure. "Henry."

He nodded approval, greeted Denver and she was finished, able to move on into the sumptuous foyer, still alive, still intact, welcomed as a new Winfield into the fold.

And what a fold! Chandeliers, rich Oriental rugs, original paintings, exotic woods, flowers, servers passing drinks and hors d'oeuvres, a string quartet in a small raised alcove toward the back of the massive living room ahead, the house was the stuff of fantasy. Lindsay couldn't imagine growing up in this life or having anything resembling a normal rough-and-tumble childhood in a place like this. And yet, the three Winfield granddaughters were in many ways better adjusted for normal life than she was, and their home on Hawthorn Lane was nearly as grand as this.

"Lindsay!" Brooke hurried over the parquet floor from a room to the left, stunning in a clingy scarlet gown with a gathered halter neckline and sexy yet tasteful keyhole front. The kind of dress made for a tall woman with zero figure flaws like Brooke. Behind her was David, looking devastating and vaguely uncomfortable in a tux that emphasized his powerful athlete's body.

"Hi, Brooke." She embraced her sister, for once not feeling odd or self-conscious exchanging hugs. Seeing Brooke's familiar face was like a miracle in the foreign surroundings.

"I was determined to be at the entrance when you

arrived, but Mr. Somebody-or-Other just had to see me and then Mrs. Somebody-Else just had to tell me about her vacation in Costa Rica and so on and I got trapped. How did it go?"

Lindsay didn't have to ask what she meant. "They both held their noses and said, 'Ew, who let *this* trash in?'"

Brooke giggled, while David opened his eyes wide. "Wait, that's what they said when I came in. Are we related?"

"Who? What?" Joey appeared behind Lindsay, soft and feminine in an emerald-green silk dress, sleeveless and softly draped and gathered around the bodice and neckline. Behind her, Sebastian, grinning and equally handsome as David. All men should be required to wear tuxes at least once a week.

"Lindsay passed muster." Brooke grinned knowingly at her sister.

Joey's brows raised. "Was there any doubt?"

"They were very sweet to me."

"Where's Katie?" Joey looked around, catching the eye of a passer-by and giving a little wave. "She was supposed to meet us here."

"There's Liam." Brooke motioned toward the also devastating Liam making his way through the swelling throng of guests. "Hi, Liam, where's Katie?"

"Hi, Brooke. Hi, the rest of you. Katie's been nabbed by a woman who desperately needs to tell the entire story of her childhood." He touched the knot of his bow tie. "And I need a drink."

As if on cue, a waiter passed with a tray of champagne glasses, each with a red sparkling heart at the bottom that looked like a ruby.

Lindsay wasn't entirely sure it wasn't.

"Perfect, thank you." Liam lifted two glasses off the tray. "I'll take a pair."

"As long as one is for me." Katie beamed a greeting around the circle, sexy and chic in a black beaded halter dress that plunged carefully down to her navel, her hair up in a sleek French twist. "So have you told her yet?"

"Of course not, we've been waiting for you."

Lindsay's stomach twisted. "Told who what?"

"You. The news." Joey winked. The rest of the circle grinned knowingly.

Lindsay glanced at Denver, who was looking terrifically pleased with himself. "You're in on this?"

"I might be."

"Oy." Lindsay rolled her eyes. "Okay, what now. We have a long-lost brother who was kidnapped by aliens?"

"Ooh, good one," Katie said.

Brooke raised her glass. "Here's to Chassy…"

Lindsay raised her glass along with everyone else, but her heart squeezed painfully, and she fixed her gaze on the polished floor. Poor Chassy.

"…and its new investors."

"New who?" Her eyes shot up to the faces of Brooke, Joey and Katie. "What investors?"

"Us." Katie grinned. "And before you get all Lindsay-like and tell us we can't, we're telling you we can and we will."

"And you should know by now how far trying to

thwart a Winfield woman gets you." Liam pursed his lips in a silent hoo-boy whistle that got him an elbow dig from Katie.

"The bar means a lot to us too, Lindsay." Brooke leaned into David. "After all, without Martinis and Bikinis—"

"And all those kinky dares you made us do—" Joey winked at Sebastian.

"We never would have met the loves of our lives." Katie stole a quick kiss from Liam.

Lindsay gaped. How could she let them decide something about her business without…

She sighed. Okay. They won. It was the perfect solution. She needed the money. They had it. For once she'd accept help graciously without fussing first, as much as she wanted to.

Beside her, Denver stroked her back. "What do you think, Lindsay?"

"It's… I'm overwhelmed. Thank you." She made eye contact around the circle, hoping each person could see how much his or her belief in the bar—and in her— meant. "But I don't know if you realize how hard it was not to object."

"We can imagine." Joey held up her hand. "Oh, I keep wondering but never remember to ask when I'm around you. Why did you name the place Chassy?"

Lindsay blushed. "You won't believe it. Even Denver doesn't know this one."

"Uh-oh." He nudged her. "Do I want to?"

"My real name, the name my adoptive parents gave

me, and which I was known by until I left home was…"
She let the expectation build. "Chastity."

A loud snort from Joey. Beside Joey, another one,
from Katie. Then it was Brooke's turn. Lindsay winked
and grinned, and the women burst out laughing while
the men had the good sense to act as if they weren't sure
what was going on.

"Well." Brooke giggled, face flushed, allowing
David to replace her glass of champagne. "What a
charming name."

"And so appropriate."

"I thought so too, that's why I got rid of it." She
gestured with her glass. "Buying the bar was like
starting over."

"Regaining your virginity."

"I hope you were gentle, Denver."

Another wave of giggles.

"Here's to our big sister Chastity!" Brooke lifted her
champagne toward Lindsay and the rest of the circle
followed suit.

"Wait, Brooke, there's something in your gla—"
Katie gasped and clapped her hand over her mouth.

"Oh my gosh. David. Oh my gosh." Brooke stared
at her champagne glass, her face flushing further. At the
bottom, churning with bubbles, instead of the fake ruby
was a very real diamond ring. Brooke turned to David,
kissed him twice fiercely and beamed at her sisters.
"He asked me last night and said he was sorry he didn't
have the ring yet. Like I cared. We were planning to
announce it today but this is perfect. Thank you, David."

She glanced furtively at the surrounding guests, then kissed him again, another peck on the lips.

"I don't think so, Ms. Winfield." David grabbed her and planted one on her that lasted a good thirty seconds while the rest of the circle cheered.

This event, of course, attracted attention, and soon the blissed-out couple was surrounded by well-wishers including Brooke's grandparents, Evelyn and Henry.

More people pressed forward. Lindsay stepped instinctively back, feeling Denver's solid presence next to her until she was on the fringe, which suited her. Except then Joey noticed she'd been pushed out and hauled her back into the fray. The next hour was introduction after introduction, explanation after explanation. Apparently Evelyn and Henry had held some kind of Winfield powwow and decided the truth would be easier to keep straight than some more socially acceptable explanation for Lindsay's presence. Details were kept to a minimum, and the word *escort* was definitely not part of the story. Lindsay was aware all eyes weren't welcoming, and that tongues would be wagging all over when people went home, which made her even more touched and grateful that Evelyn and Henry decided to out her.

However, after an hour of smiles and small talk, thrilled as she was for Brooke and David, Lindsay was worn out, not sure she could stand having to get through the sit-down dinner, the dancing and now that she was public, being the center of more speculation and gossip.

"Want to go for a walk?"

"You read my mind." She turned to Denver and the

second she met his eyes, her fatigue fell away and she started smiling. "You don't think they'd miss us?"

"In this crowd?" He gave her a c'mon-be-serious look that made her smile turn to a grin. "I'll tell Liam where we're going."

He talked quickly with Liam, the nearest of their group available, who pointed to a room, made a turning motion with his hand, then winked and gave Denver a thumbs-up.

"This way." Denver led her through a library, a solarium, another sitting room—did this house ever end?—and out a side door onto a moonlit terrace. Strains of the quartet filtered through a window open a crack to let fresh air into the overcrowded rooms. The patio was chilly but blissfully silent and open.

"Oh, this is nice. What did you tell Liam?"

"That we wanted to make out." He winked and held out his arms. "Dance with me?"

"I'd love to." She went to him, loving the strong solid feel of him pressed against her. They swayed slowly to the faint strains of what sounded like "Moonglow." "You didn't really say that to Liam, did you?"

"Why not? It's the truth." He kissed her, his lips warm in the damp night air, his hands wandering over her back. "So what do you think about all these engage-ments going on?"

"It's wonderful. I'm so happy for all of them. Three in one year in one family! That's got to be some kind of record."

"Possible." He danced her under what was undoubtedly a gorgeous rose arbor in the summer, the white painted lattice now bare and waiting for spring. "I was wondering…"

"Mmm?" She moved close to him, absorbing his warmth, her dress not made for February outdoors, even on a warm night. His arms came around her tighter; he pressed his cheek to her hair.

"What if there were four?"

Her feet stopped moving; she held still in his embrace. "Four?"

"The number after three. Before five."

Lindsay lifted her head from his shoulder. He was gazing at her with so much love in his eyes she was suddenly quite sure she'd never be cold again. "I—that would—I mean…"

"I don't want to upstage Brooke and David tonight, so this is just for you and me, Lindsay. Will you marry me?"

"Oh. Yes. I…yes. I mean…*yes.*"

He grinned, let out a laugh that sounded like pure happiness and kissed her as if he'd never stop. "So that's a yes?"

"Yes. And yes. And also yes." She laughed too, unable to keep that much joy silent. Who would have thought a year ago, two years ago, five years ago, ten, that her life could possibly have turned out like this? That the love she'd fantasized about as a child would be hers, not only from a family she couldn't possibly have imagined, but from a man as incredible as Denver?

The heroine of *A Little Princess* had nothing on her. Denver had helped transform her from a life of emotional poverty to one of untold richness. And she had no doubt in the years ahead, she'd keep the transformation going.

"I have something for you."

"Oh?" She expected a jeweler's box, but was so out of her mind with bliss that she wasn't the slightest bit disappointed when he handed her a rolled-up piece of paper, tied with a ribbon.

She untied and unrolled it, then squinted to make out the black type.

Run away from the party with the guy in front of you and make love in his car in the Winfield parking lot instead of sitting down to a fancy uncomfortable dinner with too many people you don't know.

Lindsay looked up at him coyly, eyes sending mischief, tipping her head to one side so her hair fell behind her bare shoulder. "Why on earth should I do something like that?"

He grinned and looked her up and down in a sexy slow way that had her heating up already, now and for the rest of her life.

"Because I double Martini Dare you."

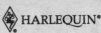

☒ HARLEQUIN®

INTRIGUE®

THRILLER—
Heart-pounding romance and suspense that will thrill you long into the night....

Experience the new THRILLER miniseries beginning in March with:

WYOMING MANHUNT

BY

ANN VOSS PETERSON

Riding horseback through the Wyoming wilderness was supposed to be the trip of a lifetime for Shanna Clarke. Instead she finds herself running for her life. Only rancher Jace Lantry can help her find justice—and serve revenge.

*Available in March
wherever you buy books.*

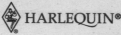

HARLEQUIN®
Blaze™

COMING NEXT MONTH

#381 GETTING LUCKY Joanne Rock
Blush

Sports agent Dex Brantley used to be the luckiest man alive. But since rumors of a family curse floated to the surface, he's been on a losing streak. To reverse that, he hooks up again with sexy psychic Lara Wyland. Before long he's lucky in a whole new way!

#382 SHAKEN AND STIRRED Kathleen O'Reilly
Those Sexy O'Sullivans, Bk. 1

When Gabe O'Sullivan describes his friend Tessa Hart as a work in progress, it gets Tessa to thinking. She's carried a torch for Gabe forever, but maybe now's the time to light the first spark and show him who's really ready to take their sexy flirting to the next level!

#383 OFF LIMITS Jordan Summers

Love happens when you least expect it. Especially on an airplane between Delaney Carter, an undercover ATF agent, and Jack Gordon, a former arms dealer. With their lives on the line, can they find a way to trust each other… once they're out of bed?

#384 BEYOND HIS CONTROL Stephanie Tyler

A reunion rescue mission turns life-threatening just as navy SEAL Justin Brandt realizes he's saving former high school flame Ava Turkowski. Talk about a blast from the past…

#385 WHAT HAPPENED IN VEGAS… Wendy Etherington

For Jacinda Barrett, leaving Las Vegas meant leaving behind her exotic dancer self. Now she's respectable…in every way. Then Gideon Nash—her weekend-she'll-never-forget hottie—shows up. Suddenly she's got the urge to lose the clothes…and the respectability!

#386 COMING SOON Jo Leigh
Do Not Disturb

Concierge Mia Traverse discovers a body in the romantic Hush hotel, which is booked for a movie shoot. Detective Bax Milligan is assigned to investigate and keep Mia under wraps. Hiding out with her in a sexy suite is perfect—except for *who* and *what* is coming next.…

HBCNM0208